# Nā Akua

CLAYTON SMITH

*Nā Akua* is a work of fiction. The characters, incidents, and dialogue are drawn from the author's imagination and are not to be construed as real. Any resemblance to actual events or persons, living or dead, is entirely coincidental.

Printed in the United States of America

First Printing, 2016

ISBN 978-0-9965121-6-9

Library of Congress Control Number: 2016914002

Dapper Press
www.DapperPress.com

*For Paula, my mana and my aloha.*

# A Glossary of Select Hawaiian Words and Phrases

&

**'Awa** – Hawai'ian name for the kava plant, the roots of which are used to make a drink with anesthetic and euphoriant properties

**Akua** – A singular god or goddess (plural: nā akua)

**Ali'i** – The hereditary line of rulers; a king

**Aloha** – Hello; goodbye; love and affection; the breath of life

**E kala mai ia'u** – "I'm sorry."

**Haole** – Someone from the mainland United States, often interchangeable with "white person," sometimes derogatory

**He akuahanai ka rama** – "Rum is a poisonous god."

**He mea 'ole** – "You're welcome" (*also*: He mea iki)

**Ho'okupu** – A gift given in exchange for spiritual energy; can refer to the intention behind the gift as well

**Huaka'i pō** – The Night Marchers, a legendary tribe of ghosts who were once ancient Hawaiian warriors who now roam the islands, searching for a way into the next life

**Hûpô** – Ignorant or foolish; unintelligent

**Kö aloha lä 'ea, kö aloha lä 'ea** – "Keep your love, keep your love."

**Kohola** – A whale

**Kupua** – A group of trickster demigods

**Kupuna** – A title of respect for a grandparent or an elder

**Mahalo** – "Thank you."

**Mahalo nui loa** – "Thank you very much."

**Mahina** – The moon

**Makuakāne** - Father

**Mana** – Spiritual energy; a healing power

**Mo'o** – Mythical shape-shifting lizards that are extremely powerful and can change their appearance at will; sometimes depicted as dragons

**Mo'olelo** – A story or legend

**Mujina** – In Japanese folklore, a badger demon, sometimes presented as a faceless ghost (or a "noppera-bō"); mujina sightings have been reported in Hawai'i since the 1950s

**'Ohana** – Family; a notion often extended beyond blood relatives

**Pali** – A cliff (*plural*: nā pali)

**Pelapela** – Filthy; dirty (*slang*)

**Pili** – A long, coarse Hawaiian grass

**Pua'a** – A pig or boar

**Shaka** – A hand gesture that means "hang loose," which is formed by closing one's fist and extending the thumb and the pinky finger (*slang*)

**Tūtū** – A title of respect for a grandparent or an elder

# Nā Akua

# Chapter 1

Grayson had been drunk before, but never in Hawai'i.

It was a good place to be drunk—a *very* good place…much better than his hometown of St. Louis, in fact, because even though St. Louis was a perfectly respectable place to overindulge, Missouri didn't smell like pineapple and plumeria blossoms, while Hawai'i most certainly did. The ever-present and heady aroma in the salty ocean air added a certain dizzying *je ne sais quoi* to Gray's whole situation, making it depressing but invigorating instead of just plain old depressing.

"I am going to bottle this smell," Gray decided out loud, proclaiming it to the palm trees as they swayed delicately in the midnight breeze, "and I am going to get so, so rich."

Maui was breathtaking, and Gray wondered why he'd never visited Hawai'i before. He'd been to all sorts of exotic vacation islands in his life, but not a single one of them approached the incredible beauty of this Maui night. His resort sprawled along a quiet beach, and the view from his spot on the hotel's expansive deck was snipped straight out of a postcard. The moon hovered in a Navy blue sky, floating high above the sloping, hulking form of the island Lāna'i that rose from the water on the horizon, solemn and peaceful and shaded dark gray by the night. Perfectly haphazard palm trees framed the image, lit from below by the resort's gentle lights, and the aqua glow of the meandering hotel pool only served to make the ocean more stunning in its variegated ultramarine, with a rippling white ribbon of light trailing the moon and splashing quietly onto the sandy beach.

"Come find me in Maui," Gray whispered, imagining the postcard headline unfurling in delicate white script across the corner of the scene. Then he cried a little bit, even though he'd promised himself he wouldn't, because it was all just so stupid and sad.

"Here's to you, moon," he said, hoisting his half-empty Mai Tai to the sky and giving the ice a little shake. "*La luna*," he added, in case the moon spoke Spanish.

There was a slice of pineapple squeezed onto the rim of the cup, and he pushed it to the side with his tongue, then managed to get his mouth around the straw on only the third try. The ice was well on its way past the point of melting, and his Mai Tai was now more water than rum. Gray made a sour face, then gave up on the straw and drank the rest down the old-fashioned way. He'd tossed out the last three Mai Tais when they'd gotten watery like this, but now he was drunk, and water was important at this stage; his instincts told him so…or maybe it wasn't his instincts but the ever-present voice of his older sister, who was never game for letting Gray have too much fun, but maybe she wasn't wrong, and water was a good thing, and he drank it down now, and so this rum-water was saving his life, and he needed it, and besides, the quicker he drank it, the quicker he could order another round, and he sensed he wasn't too many more little pineapple slices away from forgetting the thing he'd been foolish enough to think he could get away from here, in this place, on his own, without her.

"I...should slow down," he said, as his thoughts railroaded themselves off the tracks of his mind. Then he waved his arms to catch the attention of the pool bartender below, raised the glass, and rattled the ice to signal for another. The bartender frowned and made a big show of looking at his watch, which was sort of insulting, really, because Gray knew the bar didn't close for another twenty minutes, and hadn't he left that ungrateful jerk fifteen dollars in tips already that night? He shook his glass harder, and the bartender frowned harder, then Gray frowned as hard as *he* could, then the bartender frowned as hard as *he* could, but in the end, there could be only one victor, and the bartender, with no other real option, caved. He gave Gray an annoyed little wave of acquiescence and went to work fixing another rummy delight.

"I am the master of my glass," Gray said proudly, admiring the moon through the curved sides of his cup, "and I will not be denied."

He leaned forward and propped his elbows on the deck's slim iron railing. The breeze stiffened, and he closed his eyes as the salty pineapple-and-plumeria wind rushed against his skin. *This is good,* he thought. *This is what forgetting smells like.* And he wondered if it was true.

"Beautiful, isn't it?"

Gray was so startled by the sound of another voice that he squeezed his glass right out of his own hands. He grasped for it as it bobbled for a few seconds, but the glass was sweating, and his hands were clumsy, and ultimately it went spinning out of reach, its wet, sickly ice raining down on a pair of midnight lovers strolling along the pool below. The woman shrieked; the man brushed off his shirt and scowled up at the drunk guy above. Gray just shrugged and smiled a bit, and he hoped it was enough.

The new voice at his side laughed. It was a sweet laugh, cheerful and easy and decidedly female. When she spoke, the sound was fine crystal in the moonlight: "Sorry about that."

"It's okay. I was done with that one," Gray said, working hard to keep the slur out of his voice. "I threw it over on purpose." He stared straight ahead at the ocean, focusing on the thin white lines that appeared along the tops of the cresting waves in the deep blue darkness. This was something else he was determined to do: avoid all women for the entire trip, and maybe for the rest of his life. He wasn't doing a very good job of it so far. He'd spoken to three female flight attendants, a female car rental agent, a female check-in employee, and two female housekeepers since leaving St. Louis. But, hey—it was never too late to start doing better. So he kept staring at the waves and not at the woman who had sidled up next to him, and who smelled like vanilla and coconut oil and…something else he couldn't place. But it made his toes tingle in the strangest and most extraordinary way.

"It makes you wonder why they ever bothered inventing trash cans." She had a soft Hawai'ian lilt, which made each word sound painfully hand-crafted.

"I've never used one in my life," he replied.

"Are you here with the insurance group?" she asked.

Gray's elbows slipped on the railing, and his arms shot forward, slamming his armpits down on the iron edge. He grunted and tried to roll with it, spreading his arms and pressing his chest against the rail. "The who-what?" he asked.

He refused to look at her, but from the corner of his eye, he saw a sun-kissed arm reach up and point over at a group of middle-aged men on the pool deck below. They all wore polos tucked into khakis that were held up by glaringly black belts, and each one was trying his best to laugh louder than the others. "Oof. No," he soured.

"No, I didn't think so," the voice said, honey dripping down its crystal edges. "You don't have the insurance look."

Gray snorted. "What look do I have?"

"Hmmm." The woman twirled around and propped her elbows against the railing. "If I had to guess, I'd say...part-time vagrant."

Gray laughed, a loud explosion of scorn and amusement wrapped up into one big bundle of noise. "It's an option," he admitted. "I might stay in Hawai'i and never work again and be homeless and catch fish by hand and light some fires and be king of the sea." His words were actually making a surprising amount of sense, all things considered, and he mentally congratulated himself.

He swore he could hear the woman smile. "So," she said. "Can I ask what you are looking at?"

Gray raised an eyebrow at the ocean. "Looking at?" he said.

"Well, we're talking, but you're not looking at me, so you must be looking at *something* worthwhile."

Gray bit his bottom lip and resolved to just stop talking.

It worked for several seconds, until the woman prodded, "Are you not?"

Why couldn't anything be easy? Gray sighed. "I *am* looking at something, and that something is...nothing."

"You're looking at nothing?"

"Correct."

"And that nothing is better than looking at, say...the waves crashing on the beach? Or the moon? Or me?" Gray could sense her moving closer. He cleared his throat and focused even harder on nothing at all. "Or maybe," the woman continued, because she was obviously a terrible brute who refused to take a hint, "at this kind-looking man who is offering you a drink?"

"What?" Gray said with a start. He jerked up from the deck railing and became suddenly aware of the bartender from the deck below, who had brought his fresh Mai Tai up to the deck and was impatiently shoving it into Gray's chest. "Oh! Thank you. This is... okay, this is great." He took the drink in both hands and cradled it gently to his mouth. He sipped. Then he spat. "Did you put any rum in this at all?!" he cried, but the bartender, who was already retreating back down to the pool bar, gave a curt flick of his hand, and their conversation was apparently done. Gray guffawed as hard as he could. "Well," he said, in his most affronted voice, "how do you like that? I just charged my room for the world's most expensive pineapple juice."

"You know, the Mai Tai was originally made with lime juice," the woman said.

Gray buried his face in his hand. "Oh, come on," he whispered.

"What?"

"It's just...it's very, very hard to not look at you when you say such attractive things."

The woman coughed. "You're...attracted to lime juice?"

"What? That is...that is not what I meant at all!" Gray closed his eyes and finally turned to face his companion. "Cocktail knowledge is an excruciatingly attractive trait, and I'm sure you know that absolutely completely." He let his eyes open slowly, and the second he saw her, his heart sank.

Because *of course* this woman was exotic.

*Of course* this woman was entrancing.

*Of course* this woman, whom he shouldn't even have looked at in the first place, was more beautiful than even the moon, now slowly sinking toward Lāna'i and dazzling the ocean with its elegance and charm.

"Are you a witch?" he heard himself whisper.

The woman laughed, a symphony of wind chimes in the warm summer breeze. She shook out her long, black hair; it cascaded down the back of her red silk floral dress, which clung gently to the curves of her, with a long tail fluttering out behind her in the wind, a flag marking the place where the proud form of female perfection stood. She wore a large flower tucked behind her ear, one unlike any Gray had ever seen. Instead of petals, the blossom bore a fist of deep red spikes, which made it look more like a sea urchin than a flower, aside from the dark green stem that anchored it in her hair. But even the color of the prickly red spires paled in comparison to her pomegranate lips, and her dark, acorn eyes blazed in the moonlight. "Not that I am aware of," she confided, leaning in close, "though to be honest, I would be surprised if you found any witches here at all. They aren't really a Hawai'ian thing."

Gray blinked. Then he blinked again. "You're so beautiful, I hate it," he said.

The woman coughed hard, like she was choking on something, and for a second, Gray thought maybe he'd killed her with his awkwardness. But she pressed her brown hand to her chest and cleared her delicate throat, and the fit passed. "I guess I will take that as a compliment," she said with a smile that must have made even *la luna* dizzy with its gentle grace.

"I meant it as one," Gray sighed, disappointed. He'd hoped she'd be wrecked, unsightly, ruined, scarred—maybe a disfigured burn victim or a horribly malformed abomination of natural cause. But instead, she was flawless in a way that redefined the word in his brain, and he was all the more depressed for it.

It wasn't supposed to be like this.

He took a long sip from his Mai Tai. He thought about going to bed.

"Well, it's an incredibly nice thing to say, even if it causes you such discomfort," she said, and Gray swore he saw a slight blush bloom to life beneath her cheeks…but her Hawai'ian skin was so perfectly chestnut, it was impossible to tell. "*Especially* if it causes you such discomfort," she corrected herself, and Gray decided to maybe just throw himself over the deck because he wasn't sure he could handle such sweetness from a beautiful, mysterious, suddenly-materializing woman. She had apparated out of nowhere, and just like that, his heart was spinning again, reeling off a course that had already sent it hurtling out in the wrong direction, and was "apparate" even a real word, or did J. K. Rowling just invent it and make him believe it was an acceptable thing to think?

Life was hard when the rum was flowing, and at that moment, Gray knew it better than anyone.

"It's not you," he said sadly, resuming his slumped perch on the railing of the patio and running his thumb against the sweating glass. "It is infinitely me."

The woman nodded slowly and tapped her fingers against the railing. "So," she said. Gray wondered desperately what it would take to just make her go away. "You're a part-time vagrant and a full-time romantic. What brings you to Kā'anapali?"

"What…is Kā'anapali?" asked Gray. He was certain that he'd seen the moniker on a Google Map or two but he'd disregarded it in the interest of the much-easier-to-pinpoint "Maui."

The woman raised an eyebrow. "This beach?" she said. Something about her tone suggested that she might suspect Gray of being not just a drunken fool, but a *habitual* drunken fool. "The beach that we're looking at right now?"

"Oh." Gray shuffled his feet and sipped casually from his drink. "*That* Kā'anapali."

"Yes." The woman smiled again. "What brings you to *that* Kā'anapali?"

Gray sighed. His head drooped down between his elbows, and he turned the Mai Tai around nervously between his hands. "Honestly?" he said, his voice muffled by the railing.

The woman gave another laugh. "I don't see why not," she said, and it was such a sincere way of phrasing things that Gray just wanted to die.

He took a deep breath and thought maybe if he just held it in, he could quietly asphyxiate here on the patio, and that would be all right. But physiology kicked in a few seconds later, and he exhaled. "I'm on my honeymoon."

"Ah." She nodded sagely. "And is it customary for the groom to leave his bride so he can go drink alone by the ocean?"

Gray's head drooped even further. He pressed his forehead against the cool metal. The world was starting to spin, and he wanted to get off the ride. "I don't have a bride," he said quietly.

The woman nodded thoughtfully. "We may have different definitions of 'honeymoon,'" she decided.

Gray rocked his head from side to side, rolling it along the banister. "No," he said, "we probably don't." He stood straight up, gave his head a brisk shake, and turned to face the woman, and the truth of his new reality. "I was supposed to get married yesterday. To Lucy. Her name was Lucy. I guess it still is Lucy. Technically. Isn't that a nice name?"

"It is...a beautiful name," the woman said carefully, her voice stilted, hesitant.

"Almost 200 people showed up to the ceremony," Gray continued. "I was one of them. She...was not. Change of heart. I guess." He shook his glass, though the clinking of the ice was barely audible over the crashing surf below. "That's what her text said. 'Change of heart.' Two hundred people at the church, but not one Lucy. I was supposed to have a bride, but now I don't." He raised his shoulder and rubbed it against his eye. His shirt came away splotched with water and salt. "But this was booked," he said, gesturing toward the hotel, "it was paid for. Most of it, anyway. So here I am. On my honeymoon. But no honey. It's a...a solo-moon? Or just a moon, maybe." He let out another sigh as his eyes focused on nothing. "Yes. I'm alone like the moon. I am just a *la luna*," he decided. "A sad *la luna*."

They stood quietly on the deck, the cool pineapple breeze blowing between them. Finally, the woman cleared her throat and spoke. "You know, in Hawai'i, we have a saying: '*Kō aloha lā 'ea, kō aloha lā 'ea.*'"

"Does it mean, 'Throw yourself in the ocean, for all is lost'?"

The woman laughed her wind chime laugh. "The opposite, I think. It means, 'Keep your love, keep your love.' Sometimes life grows very difficult. There are many obstacles, and our hearts are easily injured. But you must keep your love, keep your *aloha*, because if that can persevere, life will always be worth living. *Kō aloha lā 'ea, kō aloha lā 'ea.*"

Gray felt his lips curl up into a little smirk. "So many vowels can't possibly be wrong."

"Nor can so many Hawai'ians," she smiled. "We are a very wise and introspective people."

Gray peeled himself off the patio railing and extended his free hand toward the woman. "I'm Grayson. Grayson Park."

Now it was the woman's turn to smirk. "Your name sounds like a beach," she said.

"And what does your name sound like?"

She took his hand in hers and gave it a gentle squeeze. "It sounds like Hi'iaka. It is very good to meet you, Grayson Park."

He felt a strange heat emanate from her palm and warm his fingers. It traveled up through his elbow, past his shoulder, until his entire arm began to melt and his chest began to glow with sunlight. The woman's eyes were pools of the richest Kona coffee; her cascading hair glistened like onyx, and the curve of her lips pulled on the pieces of his struggling heart and molded them back together into a sweet, sloping shape that was completely and utterly her own. "Call me Gray," he said weakly.

"I will," she smiled, holding his gaze. "Gray."

He let go of her hand, and the warmth of his arm began to evaporate like rain.

"Do you, um…can I—can I get you a drink?" he stammered. He leaned over and waved at the bartender below, who suddenly became extremely rapt in the drying of glasses and not at all in the recognition of the drunken guest on the patio above. "This guy…" Gray grumbled to himself.

But Hi'iaka shook her head and laid a hand on his arm. "No, thank you. We have another saying in Hawai'i: *he akuahanai ka rama.*"

"'We only drink Mai Tais made with lime'?" he guessed with a grin.

"No. 'Rum is a poisonous god.'"

Gray coughed. "Well that one gets straight to the point."

"It does," she agreed.

The insurance agents on the pool deck began to gather themselves up and shamble back into the lobby, slapping each other on the back and fidgeting with their waistbands. The bar was closing, and the other vacationers were shuffling off to their rooms. Gray looked down at the half-empty drink in his hand. Then he set it down on the ground, away from his feet. "I'll get that later," he promised.

"I'm sure you will," she teased.

"Hey, can I ask you a question?"

"Mm," she nodded.

"I don't think it's an inappropriate question, but judgment is hard right now, so I apologize if it sounds weird or offensive, but… can I ask what *you're* doing here?"

Hi'iaka closed her eyes and smiled into the night. She leaned against the railing. Watching her dress shift against her curves, Gray thought his knees might actually turn to water. "I'm standing on a lanai enjoying the breath of Maui and a surprisingly intimate conversation with a kind yet drunk stranger," she said.

"No, I mean—" Gray stopped, and he laughed. "I am kind and drunk, and kind *of* drunk. That's funny." She smiled a very genuine, if placating, smile. "But I mean…you're a local. Right? You're Hawai'ian. You have a lot of sayings to back that particular assumption up. So why are you *here*? At a vacation resort filled with 800 happy couples, a group of badly-dressed insurance salesmen, and one sad drunk?"

"Ah. That is a good question."

"And not offensive," he pointed out.

"And not offensive," she agreed. Then she leaned in closer and whispered conspiratorially, "I'm here because I am hiding from someone."

"Oh!" he said, startled. "Intrigue!"

Hi'iaka nodded. "Yes. Of the highest order."

"And who is this dastardly someone?"

Hi'iaka shrugged. "I'm not sure."

Gray frowned. "You're not sure."

"I'm not sure."

"But you *are* hiding from someone…"

"Oh, yes."

"Someone who's looking for you."

"That's right."

"But you don't know who that someone is."

"That is also right."

"But you're *sure* that someone is *actually* looking for you, and you want to hide from said someone."

She nodded. "Very sure."

Gray squeezed his eyes shut and tried to will himself to sobriety. He had a suspicion that perhaps he would understand things a little better if he'd skipped the last two or three cocktails. "Okay, I'll bite," he said, giving up. "How do you know someone is looking for you if you don't know who that someone is?"

Hi'iaka filled her lungs with the pineapple-plumeria wind. "Because I saw it in a dream," she said.

Gray's eyebrows pinched together. "A dream?"

"Mm. Each of the last twelve nights, a man has pursued me across the islands, his face and shoulders hidden by a long, black veil. The first night, he chased me through the lehua forest, running hard, his shoulders snapping off limbs and blossoms in his path. The second night, I fled across the orange lava flows of Kīlauea, and he followed me, the ground hissing under his feet. The third night, he almost caught me in the coffee fields of Kona, and if not for an untended root in the earth that snagged his ankle, he would have had me. Every night it has been like this, to Kahoʻolawe, and Lānaʻi, and now here, to Maui. In the evenings, he chases me; when I wake up, I run. I do not know who he is, but he is coming for me…I can feel him getting closer even now. Tomorrow, I'll run away to Molokaʻi and see if he finds me there."

She stopped and gave Gray a shy, sideways glance. He became acutely aware of the fact that his eyes had peeled themselves open wider than he thought human eyes could go. He shook his head to push some air to his brain and forced himself to blink. "All I ever dream about is standing naked in front of a roomful of people," he said.

Hiʻiaka smiled. "Perhaps you should follow *your* dreams to literal ends," she said, tilting her head wryly and nudging him in the arm with her shoulder.

Gray's face grew hot, the air was suddenly ten degrees warmer, and he wished he hadn't set his glass down so he'd have something to fidget with. His hands were suddenly three times their normal size and too clumsy to just hang there like coconuts, so he tried holding them in different positions: on his hips, in his pockets, crossed, folded, behind his back, on his head, and, as a desperately last-ditch effort, tented in front of his chest.

"I'm sorry; I have embarrassed you," Hiʻiaka said, and she blushed a bit then, too. There was no mistaking it this time.

"No, no," Gray said quickly, "it's just...hands." He held them up so she could see the backs of them. "Where do they go, right?"

"Mm. Right."

Gray swallowed hard. "Um. So." He gripped the railing so hard his knuckles went white, which finally solved the problem of the awkward hands. "How long do you think you can do that? Run from some dream weirdo? What if you *never* stop having those dreams?"

Hi'iaka shrugged. "Then I suppose I will never stop running," she said. "But I think they will come to an end soon."

"Yeah? Why is that?"

"In my dreams, I am not just running away from a man...I am also running toward the full moon. I think whoever is chasing me, he must capture me before the full moon, and if I can evade him until then, I will be safe."

"Huh." Gray had never known anyone to take dreams so seriously, and he'd dated a tarot reader in grad school. He glanced up at the brilliant white moon, shimmering down on the ocean waves. "Looks pretty close," he observed.

"It will be full in three nights. Then the chase will be over, no matter what happens."

"Huh. Well. All right, then."

"All right, then," she agreed.

Gray realized something then, something that made his heart sink a little, though he really had no right to be so affected by her. "So you probably won't be here tomorrow."

She tilted her head toward the ocean and closed her eyes, as if listening for some secret confirmation from the waves. "No," she said finally, swaying like the palm trees above, "I probably won't."

"Well. That's...too bad," he said. It was lame, and it was inadequate, but it was the truth. What else could he say?

Hi'iaka opened her eyes, and they softened as she held him in her gaze. "It is too bad," she decided. "I'm enjoying our conversation very much, Grayson Park."

"So am I, Hi'iaka..." He searched his brain for her last name and realized she hadn't given one. "Which is weird, because I distinctly remember waking up this morning and swearing off all conversations with all women for the rest of my life." He thought for a second. "Or...maybe it's not weird. Maybe it's actually pretty typical."

"Perhaps it is. Do you often go back on the vows you make?"

Gray inhaled sharply. "Don't use the V-word, please," he said, wincing.

"I'm sorry."

"And no, it's not that. It's just...impossible things."

"Impossible things?"

"Yeah. My sister's always telling me I have a love affair with impossible things."

"Ah. And is it true?"

Gray shrugged. "I don't know. It's not *not* true, I guess. I went to med school, even though I was terrible at biology, and sometimes I faint at the sight of blood. But I liked the challenge of it."

"So you're a doctor?"

"Ha! No. I dropped out after one semester."

"Oh."

"Yeah. Turns out it was a little *too* impossible."

"What *do* you do, then?"

"I'm an English teacher. Pretty much the total opposite of a doctor."

Hi'iaka leaned forward and propped her chin on her arms. "And what other impossible things did you love?"

Gray considered this. "Lucy. Lucy was pretty impossible."

"Oh?"

"She was the girl who always seems higher than you, even though she's almost a foot shorter. Like she's always floating. You know? I loved her so much...but she was always *other* than me. If that makes sense."

"Other than you how?"

"Well...she was the one everybody wanted. I was the one nobody expected. I think that's why I proposed after six months. Tried to seal her in before she realized she belonged with someone a little...sharper. You know?" He gave Hi'iaka a wan smile and held his finger and thumb a sliver apart from each other. "Almost made it."

Hi'iaka blinked back the film that was threatening to form into full tears in her eyes. "*Kö aloha lä 'ea, kö aloha lä 'ea,*" she said.

"*Ko aloha lie, ko aloha lie,*" Gray agreed. He reached down and picked up his watery Mai Tai. "Do you mind?" he asked.

"Not at all."

Gray took another sip as they stood quietly, awash in the soft sounds of Kā'anapali. A slow beat of drums pounded through the air, and Gray tilted his head to listen closer. "What is that?" he asked.

"That could be one of two things. Maybe it is the drums from the luau down the beach."

"Ah." Gray had seen the signs for the hotel's luau plastered all over the property. "Makes sense."

"Or it could be the *huaka'i pō*, in which case," she said with a smile, "we are all doomed."

Gray tipped his head back and raised an eyebrow. "The *huaka'i pō*?"

"Mm. Very serious."

"And what does that mean?"

"It means the Night Marchers."

"Ah. Of course. And what, pray tell, are the Night Marchers?"

Hi'iaka lowered her voice and leaned in close, as if she were about to impart a dark and terrible secret. "The Night Marchers are an army of ghost warriors. They died in the battles to unify Hawai'i. They beat their drums and follow their torches, looking for the path to the underworld. But they will never find it. They will simply roam the islands for all eternity, forever looking."

"That sounds very serious."

"Oh, it is," she agreed. "If you look the Marchers in the eye, they will capture you and drag you into their army, and you will be doomed to march with them for the rest of time."

Gray paused. The drums continued to beat as he strained his ears to determine whether or not the sound was coming closer. "Well," he decided. "Let's hope it's the luau."

Hi'iaka laughed. "Do not worry. If it is the Night Marchers, just lie on your belly and close your eyes until they pass."

Gray inspected the floor of the deck. "Doesn't look very comfortable down there," he said.

Hi'iaka shrugged. "More comfortable than being a ghost walker."

"Ha. I guess that's probably true."

Hi'iaka smiled. Then she glanced up at the moon, and her luminous face fell.

Gray noticed the change. "Uh-oh," he said, sipping his rum-and-pineapple-flavored water. He frowned. "This is it, huh?"

"I am afraid so." Hi'iaka straightened up and smoothed her dress. "I really enjoyed meeting you, Grayson—er, Gray. I hope we will meet again."

Some strange fire kindled to life in Gray's chest, and before he could stop it, the sparks popped out of his throat as words: "Maybe you shouldn't run tomorrow. Maybe...maybe you should stay. And see what happens."

She gave him a sad smile and clasped her hands between her hips, kneading her fingers nervously. "You may not believe in dreams...but believe me when I tell you, the risk would be great."

He nodded sadly. "Yeah. I figured."

She hesitated, then reached out and laid her hand over his arm. He felt the intense heat of her touch again, and his elbow began to tingle. "Maybe we'll just wait and see what tomorrow brings," she said, her dark eyes shining. "If the day still finds me on Maui, I'll meet you here, on this lanai, tomorrow at midnight."

Gray melted into a smile. "I'd like that," he said. "And if you don't show?"

She gave him a squeeze. "Then maybe our paths will cross again beneath a whole new moon." Then, as suddenly as the breeze, she let go of his arm, spun around, and disappeared into the hotel.

Gray watched her go, his head swirling with rum and with the wonder of this woman. "See you under *la luna*," he whispered to the wind. The palm trees rustled in response, and the moon crawled closer to the horizon of Lāna'i. Gray took a deep breath, finished his overpriced drink, set the glass on the patio, and headed in to try to sleep.

# Chapter 2

Grayson welcomed death.

His mouth was as dry as bleached bone, his throat rasped and rattled for water, his stomach was slowly turning itself inside-out, and the sunlight streaming in through the balcony doors sliced deeply into the field of his brain and uprooted a chorus of mandrakes until their screams rang out through his ears and little red spots exploded through his vision.

He was seriously hung-over.

"Rum *is* a poisonous god," he mumbled to the ceiling. Then he yelled it, so the Hawai'ian Deity of the Cursed Morning After would hear and know his pain: "*Rum is a poisonous goooood!*" The people staying above him pounded on their floor. He tried to stick his tongue out at the ceiling, but it was thick and pasted to the roof of his mouth. So instead, he just glared.

*Water and coffee,* he thought. *And then, greasy breakfast.* But the thought of food crippled his stomach, and he lunged sideways so he wouldn't choke on whatever vomit might come up, and in doing so, he threw himself right over the side of the bed and crash-landed on the floor. "I just want to die," he said, but his words were muffled by the thin hotel carpet, and the Hawai'ian gods did not hear.

It took a full ten minutes for Gray to struggle to his feet, and another twenty for him to figure out the coffee maker. Every sound was a cacophony; every step was torture. But finally, *finally*, he managed to down a few glasses of water, grab the steaming cup from beneath the coffee drip, and shuffle out to the balcony. He felt sure that the brightness of the sun would explode him to ashes like a vampire, and as he eased himself down into the chair, he gave thanks for the small mercy of a room with west-facing exposure.

When his eyes had adjusted enough for the blue sky to no longer sear his vision, he blinked up at the clouds and inhaled deeply. The salty air filled his lungs, and the pale ghost of the moon had faded so much that it seemed translucent. Memories of the previous evening bumped and banged their way to the front of his brain, so he shut his eyes against the pain. He was shocked to realize how much of the surreal and magical night he remembered…and he was infinitely *less* shocked that, though he had come to Hawai'i in an attempt to forget a woman, he had somehow managed to fall for a different one he knew almost nothing about. "I am a champion of life," he muttered miserably. Then he sank down in the chair and willed the coffee to stave off his imminent death.

The morning passed slowly. Gray felt marginally less like a walking corpse after a breakfast of loco moco, which was a victory. The combination of hamburger, fried egg, brown gravy, and rice weighed down his stomach and kept it from rocking right out of his throat.

He waited near the pool bar until it opened, thinking he could use some hair of the dog, though he kept getting looks of pity from the happy couples who passed his lonely chair on the way to their tandem sunbathing. When the bar finally did open, he ordered another Mai Tai, but whoever started that "hair of the dog" nonsense was full of it, because after only three sips, he threw up in the bushes behind the towel caddy. No fewer than seven people saw him do it, and when he stood up and wiped his mouth, he saw the horror and disgust that painted their faces. Before they could fetch a hotel employee to give him five vacation demerits, or whatever they used to punish sad sack guests, Gray plunged through the bushes and forced his way through the hedge wall to the other side. He tripped on a tangle of roots and fell out of the cluster of bushes, but a lukewarm pond broke his fall, so it could have been worse. He spluttered and splashed his way to the banks and made rude hand gestures at the swans; even they were looking down at him with pity. He ran across the lawn and up the stairs, into the lobby and down the hall, past the conference rooms, and out the side door of the hotel to avoid confrontation with irate hotel employees after his performance. He wrung himself out in the parking lot next to the service entrance, then strode around to the front and walked through the main doors with his damp head held high, as if he was returning from a leisurely stroll.

*Just another fun-filled day in Hawai'i*, he thought.

After that fiasco, he decided to be a bit more conservative with the time he spent near the pool, where people would instantly, and maybe vocally, recognize him as "that guy" who'd thrown up next to the pool. He puttered around the lobby instead, sticking his head into the hotel shops that sold overpriced sunblock and honey-roasted macadamia nuts. He made small talk with the maintenance men who watered the plants in the lobby, but that, too, ran its course after they'd covered the weather, the beach, and the best places to get a good piece of fish. The only other thing he could think to discuss was his crippling loneliness, and he felt fairly certain they didn't want to talk about that.

Every time he passed a mirror, he glanced at his reflection, and every single time, he was startled that he still looked so much like himself. His brown hair was messier, his pale skin was a little tanner, and his eyes were rimmed with red, either from crying so much or from the chemicals in the swan pond. Probably both. But on the whole, he saw the familiar face of Grayson Park; things had hardly changed at all, and after everything he had gone through, he found it wholly perplexing that not a single bit of him had actually slipped away, even though he could feel himself flaking apart on the inside, little by little, like ash.

He considered heading down the beach walk, a newly paved sidewalk that wound and curled its way down Kā'anapali, slinking past the other resorts and unfurling in front of a shopping area called Whalers Village. He wasn't much for shopping, but he had a hunch that even though the rum had been a bust, something easier on the stomach—like a beer, maybe—might be just the ticket to righting his ship. With his own pool bar now more or less off-limits, he could beer-hop his way from resort to resort, all the way down the coast. But if he did that, he wouldn't be able to keep an eye on the hotel for Hi'iaka...and wasn't that *really* what today was all about—the enchanting woman he'd met in his drunken stupor the night before? If she were leaving the resort, which she almost certainly would be given their conversation, maybe he could catch her on her way out and try to persuade her to stay...and if he couldn't stop her from leaving, well, he could give her his phone number at least. Or they could make plans—*real* plans—to meet up in three or four days, after her bizarre full-moon dream-running game was over. He'd be in Maui for another week; there was no reason it couldn't happen. And if not that, then he could just tell her, just try to thank her and maybe explain to her what a strange comfort she'd been to him last night...how, like a sweet, cool breeze she had blown soothingly across the raw pain of the Lucy-shaped hole in his body.

If he left the hotel, he wouldn't get that chance.

So he sat in the lobby, trying to be inconspicuous and avoiding his unchanging reflection as he begged his head to stop hurting.

And he watched the elevators. And he watched the doors.

And he waited for Hi'iaka to appear.

And he came to miserable grips with the extraordinary fact that he had fallen in love with yet another impossible thing in the shape of a beautiful woman.

# Chapter 3

Gray checked his watch. Two minutes to midnight.

His palms were slick with sweat, so he looked around for something to dry them on, something that wasn't his shirt or his shorts. He came up empty. So he just shook them instead and hoped for the best.

He glanced nervously up at the moon—or rather, he glanced up at where the moon would be, if not for the blanket of clouds in the nighttime sky. "Come on, *la luna*," he whispered, bouncing on his toes. "Don't be a jerk."

The day had ended with a few room service beers and a pretty good pork sandwich, all of which he'd consumed from his balcony…which, he realized after five wasted hours in the lobby, actually looked out over the front entrance to the hotel. For the whole afternoon, he'd stared out at the sloping driveway, hoping to catch a glimpse of Hi'iaka. He wasn't entirely sure what he'd do if he saw her—he kept the empty beer bottles close, in case he had to start smashing them from three stories up to get her attention. But it didn't matter, in the end, because he didn't see her.

He hoped it meant she was still at the hotel.

Now here he stood, back on the lanai, feeling nervous and awkward like a high school kid praying for his prom date to show. There was no sign of her yet.

But she still had two minutes.

"So much can happen in two minutes," he told himself, swinging his arms and clicking his tongue in his cheek. "You could ride fifteen bulls in two minutes. Most people never even find the time to ride one at all."

He frowned down at his t-shirt and wondered for the fiftieth time if he should have worn a button-down.

*No way,* said a little voice in the back of his head. *She would have thought you were a total nerd.*

"Yeah, but now I look sloppy," he argued, smoothing out the cotton.

*It's not sloppy,* insisted the voice, *it's beach-casual.*

"Yeah. Beach-casual. Okay. Yeah. I'm beach-casual." He lowered his voice an octave and leaned back with his elbows on the railings. "I'm...beach-casual," he crooned, giving the empty patio a wink. Then his elbows slipped on the streaks of sweat his hands left behind, and he fell backward, his armpits slamming into the metal railing for the second time in two days. "Ow!" he whined, pulling himself up and shaking out his arms. He searched for bruises and found a pair of circular sweat stains instead. "Seriously?!" he cried, flapping his sleeves in a desperate attempt to get them to dry. "Why am I such a mess?"

*You're a beach-mess,* the voice said in the most soothing tone it could muster. Then it thought for a second. *But...man, yeah. Seriously. You're a disaster.*

"Thanks."

He looked glumly down at his watch once more. Precisely midnight.

Hi'iaka was not there.

"She's probably on beach time," he reasoned aloud, pinning his arms down at his sides so no one could see the rapidly-spreading stains around the pits. "She'll be here. Probably. I mean...right? She'll probably show."

At 12:47, he decided to call it a night.

"Impossible things," he sighed over the sound of the ocean below. "Impossible, impossible, impossible things."

He was about to walk back into the hotel when the moon broke through the clouds, washing the beach in its soft white glow. "Save it," Gray called up to the sky, shaking his head. "She's not coming."

But something caught his eye, something illuminated by the moonlight down on the beach below. It was movement of some sort that he couldn't quite make sense of. He leaned over the railing and squinted into the darkness. Something was definitely moving in the sand...

The trail of activity broke up the beach and crossed onto the hotel's lower patio. It looked like a long string snaking its way across the concrete.

It was headed for the ramp that led to the deck where Gray stood.

"What...is that?" he whispered, cocking his head to the side and furrowing his brow at the thin white thread. "Is that a...no; tapeworms only live *inside* of people. Don't they? Or...wait, *do* they?" He wished he'd continued med school for another semester. He almost certainly would have had a biology class.

The thread continued to grow as it wound around the pool deck, and soon it was twenty feet long and counting. It really did look like a tapeworm. Gray was rapt with fascination and disgust and couldn't look away. The front end of the thread reached the sloping walkway toward the deck where he stood, and in the wash of moonlight, he could see that it wasn't a thread at all, but a long, wavering line of moving, skittering *somethings*.

"What *are* those?" he muttered. He looked around for someone else, *anyone* else who might be witnessing this phenomenon spewing forth from the beach, but he was alone on the lanai. This entire end of the resort was deserted, as far as he could see. Even the bar was untended, and that was definitely not normal. He turned back to the army of single-file creatures and recoiled when he saw how much progress they'd made in the few seconds his back was turned. The head of the line was almost all the way to the top of the ramp now, and the train trailed all the way back to the beach....where it was still growing. He took a few steps backward, peering down in wonder at the tiny white creatures. He could see them clearly now; they were hideous little monsters, with vicious, snapping claws and bulging, waggling eyes as dark and black as ink. Each one skittered on five pairs of legs, with hard exoskeletons that scratched and scrabbled against the cement. They were unsightly. They were grotesque. They were...

"Sand crabs?" Grayson Park had seen many strange things in his life. He had seen a rooster do a tap dance in Texarkana. He had seen a woman set herself on fire while swallowing swords on Coney Island. He'd even once seen a cloud in the sky that looked *exactly* like fat Elvis, jumpsuit and sweat and microphone and everything, and he had the picture on his phone to prove it. But a fifty-foot line of sand crabs scuttling sideways in unison into a Hawai'ian hotel at forty-eight minutes after midnight had them all beat. He knew it, and so did his knees, which was probably why they turned to jelly the second it all computed, sending him crumpling to the patio, dazed and terribly, horribly confused.

The sound of the crabs as they drew nearer was deafening. Tiny though they were, the *clack-clack-clack* of thousands of claws on concrete could be heard over the soft roar of the ocean. The crabs reached the deck, turning at the top of the ramp. They moved straight for the spot where Gray lay collapsed on the ground. The entire army of crustaceans came for him, snapping their claws and wagging their terrible eyes. He wanted to leap to his feet, to sprint to the elevator, to run screaming to his room, to stuff towels under the door so they couldn't come in, couldn't rip the skin from his flesh and feast on his organs. But he was paralyzed, frozen in his confusion and amazement, and his traitorous body refused to re-act with either fight or flight. Instead, he lamely put up his hands, shielding his face from the pale white onslaught.

But when the head crab reached his foot, it turned to the left.

The second in line turned to the right.

The third went to the left, the fourth went to the right, and so on—left, right, left, right, so that the long line of sand crabs broke like a wave at the toe of his flip-flop and spread around him, enveloping him in a sea-life circle as the two curving columns met behind his back. When the circle was complete, the next crabs in the line split off and made a second ring just outside of the first, and when *that* circle was whole, they formed a third, and a fourth. Gray could do nothing but watch helplessly as he was surrounded by more and more sand crabs on all sides.

After a few minutes, the procession ended, and the final circle was complete. The crabs surrounded him in concentric rings more than thirty rows deep.

He finally climbed to his feet and made a full spin, gaping down at the crabs that covered the deck like a blanket. The crabs didn't move; they stared up at him with their black eyes waving on their little stalks, like they were waiting for some signal.

"What is happening?" he asked.

The crabs began to click their claws in the air. Then, on some imperceptible cue, the tiny monsters to his right broke ranks and spun open like a door, leaving a man-sized break in their crustacean wall. The crabs looked up at him expectantly. They blinked. They blinked again.

They waited.

"Is that...for me?" Gray asked, pointing at the opening. His cheeks flushed a little at the realization that he was addressing a host of sand crabs. But then again, they seemed to be the ones with all the answers. "Should I...go?"

The crabs clicked their claws. Their eyestalks bobbed.

Gray stepped through the opening.

The crabs that formed the open door broke free of formation once again. They thinned themselves into a single-file line and click-clacked their way back to the top of the ramp. When they reached it, they stopped and turned back to look at Gray. *Click-click-click* went their claws. They blinked again.

"Down there?" Gray asked, pointing at the lower patio. The eyestalks bobbed. He shook his head in weary disbelief and threw up his hands. "What the hell?" he said, stepping toward the walkway. He remembered something he'd told his students during the unit on Edgar Allan Poe the previous year, and he smiled in bewilderment. He gestured toward the crabs and the dark beach beyond and declared, "You might as well embrace the weird!"

He marched down the ramp and followed the crab line around the pool. He chanced a look over his shoulder and saw the circular mass of crustaceans unspooling itself and following him down the walkway. He whistled and shook his head. "Pretty neat trick," he murmured.

An incident from a month or so earlier popped into his head: his buddy Patrick had rounded up a few guys Gray barely knew, headed down from Chicago, picked him up in his old Impala, and driven the whole crew down to Memphis for Gray's bachelor party. It was a pretty depressing experience, all things considered, at least the parts Gray remembered. Except for Patrick, the other guys were practically strangers, and the town itself had been in something of an economic gutter. But there were definitely some highlights, and one of them presented itself as they stumbled through the Peabody Hotel that Saturday morning as a shortcut to the next bar and saw a line of trained ducks marching down the carpet and climbing into the hotel fountain. It was a strange and wonderful thing to watch, especially after a few beers, and it had left quite an impression on Gray.

He remembered those Peabody ducks now. *If you can train a duck,* he thought, *maybe you can train a crab, too.*

He set a mental reminder to give the hotel five stars on Yelp for their impressive work with crustaceans.

The crabs shuffled around the pool, waving past the deck chairs in the soft moonlight with uncanny precision. Gray followed slowly, careful not to crush any of the creatures underfoot. They led him around the edge of the pool, under a line of umbrellas, across the beach walk, and right onto the sand.

"I am *not* following you into the ocean," he warned, pulling off his flip-flops and stepping onto the beach. "I've seen *Jaws.* I know how this goes."

But the crabs stopped about halfway down the bank. They began to clump together, forming a tight collection of shells and claws that grew larger and larger as the laggards caught up and filed into place. The crab pile grew so big that Gray had to take a few steps backward just to give them more room. The last crab joined the group, and there were a few seconds of tense silence as they stood there as one, bobbing their eyestalks, clicking their claws.

And then they went to work.

They exploded into a crabby frenzy, digging furiously into the beach and flinging sand in every direction. The little white creatures swarmed over the space, their claws *thfft-thfft-thfft*ing in the dry sand. In their haste to complete their mysterious job, some climbed over the backs of others, and a few miniature scuffles broke out as Gray looked on. For a few minutes, he could see nothing but a flickering mass of tiny crabs...then, all together, they stopped their work and backed away, a wide, circular opening forming on the beach where they'd been so diligently scrambling. Gray looked down at the space they left behind.

Then he completely forgot how to breathe.

The crabs had written him a message in the sand. It was written in a neat, feminine script. It read, *Captured by the man in the black veil. Help me, Grayson. Find Pele.*

Gray shook his head slowly in disbelief.

The Peabody ducks had never done *that*.

"What is this?" he demanded, suddenly angry. He felt like someone was playing a trick on him, and he was definitely not in on it. "What *is* this?!" But the sand crabs backed away slowly from their work, dispersing across the beach. Some dug tiny caves and disappeared beneath the sand; others scooted backward and sank into the shadows of the night. And just like that, Gray was standing alone with his message in the sand.

He ruffled his hands through his hair and mopped his palms down his face. Then he stared at the writing and gave a deep sigh.

"This is the weirdest honeymoon I've ever been on."

# Chapter 4

It still didn't make any sense the next morning.

Gray had puzzled over the message all night. Delivery method aside—and the "written by a team of hyper-intelligent sand crabs" aspect was not something a person could easily just put aside—the message was...well, confusing. It was either from Hi'iaka, or it was meant to *look* like it was from her; he didn't know anyone else being chased, either literally or subconsciously, by a man wearing a black veil. But assuming it *was* from her, and assuming the man in black *was* actually real, and assuming she really *was* in trouble, and assuming he *wasn't* having the world's most prolonged stroke...how was he supposed to help her? And who the hell was Pele? Unless the soccer star had retired in Maui, Gray wouldn't even know where to start.

And then, there were the sand crabs. Those incredible, terrifying sand crabs. That was a whole sphere of unreality that Gray decided he couldn't let his brain even try to compute for fear of shutting it down entirely and spending the rest of his life as a drooling zombie mess.

"What do I do?" he said out loud as he lay in bed, hands behind his head. "What, oh what, oh what, oh what?"

After twenty minutes without a response from the ceiling, he made a decision.

ᘐ

"Of *course* I know who Pele is!" The concierge beamed from behind her massive oak desk, her smile stretching too far for her face to handle. "Don't *you*?"

Gray puffed up his cheeks with air and exhaled. "Wouldn't be asking if I did," he said, laughing to smooth the delivery, but doing so a little too loudly.

If the concierge noticed, she didn't let on. "Well, just *everyone* in Hawai'i knows about *Pele*," she said, giving him an exaggerated wink.

"Oh. Okay." Gray straightened up in his seat. "Do you know how I can get in touch with him?"

"Sure! Go throw yourself in the nearest volcano!" She slapped the desk and laughed like nothing would ever be serious again.

Gray squirmed uncomfortably in the chair. "I'm not sure I follow."

"And it's a her," the concierge continued, barreling through Gray's confusion.

"I'm sorry?"

"Pele! She's a *her*, not a *him*!"

"Oh. All right, well...what do you mean about a volcano?"

"That's where she lives!" the concierge cried, screeching with laughter. "Oh! Word to the wise: Make sure you bring her a glass of gin, or she'll melt you down to lava soup!" She burst out in an insufferable cackle.

Gray rolled his eyes. "Okay," he muttered, hauling himself to his feet. "Thanks for your help."

Her echoing laughter haunted him all the way out of the lobby.

*That's it*, he decided. *I followed the plan; I asked about Pele. But that lady was a lunatic, and it's time to let it go. And maybe go see a doctor. I might be bleeding in the brain.* He prodded his head, feeling for tender spots.

"*Psst!* Cuz!"

Gray started. He glanced around. There were a few other guests milling around the lobby, but none of them were looking at him. He shrugged and kept on toward the elevators.

The voice spoke up again. "*Cuz!*"

Gray stopped. He made a full circle, but didn't see anyone looking his way. Then he saw the leaves rustle on a nearby potted plant the size of a Buick. Crouched behind the branches, peering through the leaves, was a resort groundskeeper. "Over here," the man hissed.

After a cadre of half-sentient sand crabs, a mysterious man hiding behind a Jurassic Park fern was nothing.

Gray trotted over to the plant and peeked his head around the pot. "Are you talking to me?" he asked.

The small man in the brown and tan leaf-patterned button-down nodded enthusiastically. "Yeah, cuz. Come here."

He reached out and grabbed Gray by the front of his shirt, pulling him fully into the concealed corner behind the gargantuan plant. "Hey!"

"Shhh!" The man held a small finger to his thin lips. "Listen. You looking for Pele?"

Gray frowned. "Well...yeah..."

The little man's eyes narrowed. "Like, *Pele* Pele?" he asked.

"I have no idea," Gray whispered. "Who's Pele Pele?"

"Not Pele Pele," the groundkeeper hissed. "Like, *Pele* Pele. Like, *the* Pele. You looking for *the* Pele?"

"I am looking for *a* Pele," Gray shot back. "Right now, I will take literally *any* Pele."

"There's only one Pele I know of."

"Then that's the one I'll take."

"Ooooh, cuz." The small man let go of Gray's shirt and cocked an eyebrow. "She's a tough customer. You sure you wanna go down that road?"

"I am sure about absolutely nothing."

The groundskeeper sighed. "I can put you in touch with my cousin, Polunu. He can hook you up with Pele."

"Seriously?"

"Yep. I think so. I'm pretty sure. I mean, if anyone can do it, he can."

Gray furrowed his brow. A meeting with a stranger, set up by another stranger, was about 30% likely to end up with Gray waking up in a bathtub of ice with one kidney missing. "Am I going to get murdered here?" he asked, narrowing his eyes.

The man looked hurt. "No way," he said. "That's terrible." Then he thought about it a moment, and added, "But if you *did* get murdered in Hawai'i, it wouldn't be the worst place to die."

"Huh." Gray couldn't argue with that. "All right," he sighed. "Let's do it. Set it up." He swirled a finger through the air.

"Good, good," the groundskeeper said, nodding. He held out his palm. "Fifty bucks."

"What?!"

"You give me fifty bucks, I'll set you up."

"Fifty bucks? That's extortion!" Gray cried.

The groundskeeper thought about this. "I guess it is," he finally decided. He shrugged. "So what?"

"So what? It's illegal!" Gray hissed.

"Yeah, okay. See you 'round. Enjoy your vacation, *haole*."

He turned to leave, but Gray grabbed him by the arm. "Wait!"

The man stopped.

"Okay. Geez. Here." Gray plucked his wallet from his pocket and counted out three twenties. "You have change for sixty?"

"Nope," the groundskeeper said, swiping the bills. "Sixty is good. Now I'll even tell my cousin to be nice to you, okay?"

"Great," Gray mumbled miserably. "Thanks."

"No problem." He thumbed through the cash to make sure it all added up. Then he stuffed it in his pocket. "Listen," he said, glancing up at Gray, his eyes softening a bit. "I gotta warn you: you go see Pele, you get yourself into a whole world you don't understand. You know?"

"No," Gray said, shaking his head. "I very, very much do not know."

"No," the groundskeeper agreed. "You don't." He sighed, rested his hands on his hips, and gave his head a little shake. "I'm just saying, if you're gonna go looking for Pele, you better make sure it's for the right reason."

"I am," Gray said, and he was surprised by his lack of hesitation.

"No. Be *really* sure," the groundskeeper insisted. "You ain't never met no one like her, I promise you. This is a dangerous thing."

A chill prickled its way down Gray's spine. He shook it off and thrust his chin toward the smaller man. "I teach at a public school," he said. "I can handle anything."

"All right, cuz," the groundskeeper shrugged. "It's your funeral. Now go find a pen. I'll give you directions."

# Chapter 5

*In one quarter of a mile, your destination will be on the right.*

Gray pulled off his sunglasses and squinted through the windshield. He saw trees, and he saw some more trees, and beyond those, he saw lots more trees. But there most definitely was not a store called Mile Marker 3 Fruit & Nuts.

*You have passed your destination,* the phone's navigation voice scolded him. *Finding a new route.*

"Stupid phone," he said, giving it a good shake. But the blue line on the screen was insistent. The store was behind him. So he decided to give it one more pass.

He pulled over onto the shoulder and waited for the road to clear. Then he whipped around and drove slowly back the way he'd come, and the phone felt that this was a very good decision.

*In one thousand feet, your destination will be on the left.*

Gray slowed even more. A car zoomed up behind him and honked, and Gray waved him around. The car swerved into the oncoming traffic lane and blew past, but the driver gave him a genuine and kindly wave as he zipped around.

*Huh,* Gray thought, and he shrugged. *Hawai'i.*

The phone told him once more that he'd reached his destination, and Gray shook his head in disbelief. There was *nothing* out here on the highway. *Nothing.* He pulled over to the shoulder again and put the car in park. He peered through the window and out into the jungle. He wasn't insane. There was no Mile Marker 3 Fruit & Nuts.

There *was* a green mile marker on the side of the road. And it *was* the marker for the third mile of the road. And there also was an old, rusty VW bus with a canopy strung up along the side of it, hidden off the side of the road beneath some rainbow eucalyptus trees. And there *was* a table set up under the canopy with a few pineapples, some mangoes, a half-dozen bunches of tiny bananas, and a cardboard box holding Ziploc bags full of roasted nuts. And now that he looked carefully, he *did* see a paper bag pinned to the side of the Volkswagen that said "Fruit and Nuts" written in a hasty, scrawling hand.

"Oh my God," he whispered, pressing his forehead against the glass. "It's *George of the Jungle* out here."

He took a deep breath and gathered his courage. *This is it,* he thought. *This is the point of no return.* He could just go back to the resort, plant himself in a pool chair, keep the island drinks coming, finish out the week in Maui, and forget all about the beautiful, enigmatic woman who jabbered nonsense in the moonlight. Or he could open the car door, cross the street, present himself to the Hawai'ian van-fruit person, and get himself entangled in the weird, mystifying drama of Hi'iaka, his own personal Cinderella of the Sand Crabs.

He pictured the hotel pool. It looked beautiful. The water sparkled, the sun soaked the patio; the wind blew a sweet, cool caress against the sunbathers, and the women baked themselves from pastry white to coconut brown. It was a good place, that pool. A comfortable place. And with any luck, no one would remember him as the guy who puked behind the towel bin. And if they did, well, so what? He was on vacation.

The pool was nice. The pool was safe. But a kidnapped woman and a message written by beach creatures and a man named Polunu who sold pineapples and roasted nuts under a tarp by the side of the road…those things weren't comfortable. They were not safe. They were confusing and strange. They were way too adventurous for a vacation of heartbreak. They were epic-level complications.

He taught epics in the classroom. He knew how they ended.

He sure as hell didn't want to live one.

He shook his head and sighed. "People drown in pools all the time," he said aloud. Then he popped open the door and jogged across the road.

"Hello?" he asked uncertainly, keeping a safe distance from the fruit table and peering into the van windows as best he could. "Um…hello?"

"HOWZIT, BRADDAH?" The door to the van was thrown open, and the largest Hawai'ian man Gray had ever seen stepped out from the shadows inside. He was well over six feet tall, and almost that wide, too. He was chubby, but he was *more* than that; he was also broad and powerful. The great rolls under his chin, along his belly, under his arms…it was like they had been fitted into place, bespoke accessories of skin and fat, perfectly custom-fit for this mountain of a man. He wore his weight like a suit of armor.

Gray felt small and frail by comparison.

And pasty. He felt embarrassingly pasty, too.

The Hawai'ian man had a long, shiny mane of jet-black hair that he had piled into a knot on the top of his head. He wore baggy blue shorts and a sleeveless gray t-shirt that must have been made from the sails of some long-shipwrecked boat. A thick labyrinth of tattoos covered his upper left arm and disappeared under his shirt as they continued along his chest. They were jagged, tribal shapes that spiraled into ocean waves and tongues of fire, crisscrossed with fishing nets and long, sprawling silhouettes of lizards. He wore loose, ragged flip-flops on his feet, stained red by the dense Maui dirt.

"HOWZIT?" he boomed again, his voice a shot from a cannon.

"Sorry...what?" Gray asked, taking a few steps backward. "How...How's what?"

The Hawai'ian uncovered his teeth with a wide smile that took up the entire bottom half of his face. "I said, 'Howzit, braddah?'" he said again, in a much more manageable tone. He let loose a great laugh, and his belly bounced happily under the thin gray cotton. He held up his huge hands and rolled them through the air. "How-are-you-doing?"

"Oh. Fine. I'm fine. Good. Um...are you...?" He paused and pulled the hastily-scrawled note from the hotel groundskeeper from his pocket to double-check. "Are you...Polunu?"

"That's me! King of the fruit! Whatchoo want? I got the best pineapple on Maui, mmmm—you ain't never tasted nothing like this. I'll tell you the secret: I only plant pineapple at night, and only three full nights after a full moon. You do that, you sprinkle the ground with cinnamon, you say the blessing—boom; you grow the best pineapple on Earth." He leaned down, and Gray shivered as he fell completely into the big man's shadow. "You don't tell no one Polunu's secret, okay?"

Gray gulped. "Um. Sure. No. I won't."

Polunu winked. "Good," he said with a grin. He reached behind the table and pulled out an old, worn machete. "You try some of this goodness!" He brought the machete down hard, and Gray screamed. But Polunu wasn't swinging at him; he brought the blade down on the nearest pineapple and sliced the crown clean off. He picked up the shorn pineapple and began gently cutting away the prickly skin with the machete like a normal-sized man might peel an apple with a paring knife. "I also got these mangoes and apple bananas—they're pretty good too. You like papaya? I don't got no papaya. You come back tomorrow, you can have banana bread. Ooooo, the best banana bread on Maui, braddah—swear my life on it. Here, give this a try." He held out a piece of the freshly-cut pineapple, and Gray began to protest, but Polunu smiled his huge smile and shoved the fruit into Gray's mouth. Gray sputtered and coughed. Polunu laughed, and the earth shook with his thunder. "That first bite, it get you like *whoa!*"

"Thanks, but...I'm not here for fruit." Gray crushed the pineapple between his teeth, and a million fireworks exploded on his tongue. The pineapple was sweet, and juicy, yes, but *complex*... the taste was intensely floral, like he was eating a pineapple juice-soaked bouquet of orchids. "Wow. That is *really* good, though."

"Nighttime and cinnamon," Polunu reaffirmed, holding his hand up like he was taking an oath. "How many you want? Eight? I'll sell you eight. Very expensive," he added with a grin, "but worth it, you know?"

"No," Gray replied. "I mean, yeah, worth it, I guess, but I'm not buying any fruit."

"Oh." Polunu's face fell. "Well, maybe you're in the wrong place, then." He gestured to the van with a sweep of one massive hand. "See, this is a *fruit* stand."

"I know. I know. Um...look, this is sort of weird, but...your cousin sent me? He said you could help me."

"Which cousin?" Polunu asked suspiciously.

"Oh. Uh...I didn't get his name. He works at the Hyatt?"

Polunu nodded thoughtfully. "I got, like, ten cousins who work that job," he said. "But it's okay, they all good people. Whatchoo need?" He sat down on a blunt wooden bench behind the fruit table. It groaned and creaked under his weight, but miraculously, it did not collapse.

Gray shifted nervously from one foot to the other, then back again. "Well...this is maybe pretty strange." He took a deep breath. "But here's the deal..."

He proceeded to tell the Hawai'ian about the mysterious woman Hi'iaka, about her dream, and about the message in the sand. As he relayed the story, a huge rush of energy swelled inside of him, and he spoke faster and faster, going back for more details and peppering them into the story, spewing the words like a volcano. It was a *relief* to share the insanity of the last 36 hours with someone. It was too strange to keep it inside; it was spinning his brain, burning his neurons to a crisp, and once he opened the valve to release the pressure, it all broke loose—every bit. He talked about how Hi'iaka had smelled like coconut and vanilla, how the moon had shimmered down on the ocean like a painting, how the sand crabs had clicked their little claws and blinked their little eyes, how they'd had extraordinary penmanship for such unassuming crustaceans. He even told about how he'd vomited behind the towel bin, though it had absolutely nothing to do with the story, but it felt so good to be telling someone something that he told this person everything. And when he was done, he was sweating, and out of breath, and he felt wonderfully, immeasurably lighter.

"So I'm here because I need your help," he finished. "To find this Pele person."

Polunu stared quietly at Gray for several long seconds. The mirth had evaporated from his face, leaving behind an intensely placid mask that looked like it had been carved from wood. "So who are you?" he said at last, crossing his great arms in front of his powerful chest and raising an eyebrow. "Indiana Jones?"

"Oh. Sorry...I'm Gray. Grayson. Grayson Park."

"Grayson Park?" Polunu snorted. "That sounds like a place."

Gray nodded and silently cursed his parents, not for the first time. "It does," he agreed.

"Listen, Grayson Park. You seem like good *haole*. The best thing for you? Go back to the Hyatt. Pack your bags. Take the next plane home." He heaved himself up from the bench, and it sighed with relief. He stood up to his full height and placed one meaty paw on Gray's shoulder. "Trust me," he said, his eyes looking gravely down into Gray's. "You don't want no part of this thing you're doing."

Gray returned the larger man's stare. He saw a fierceness in Polunu's eyes, but a kindness, too. And laid over it all, a sadness that felt intensely familiar.

He sighed. "Is this about the pineapples? I'll buy the eight pineapples, okay? If you help me."

"I *am* helping you," Polunu said. "You got no idea what you stepping into."

"So I keep hearing," Gray mumbled. He felt like a child being scolded for eavesdropping on an adult's conversation. "You know, maybe if someone told me exactly *what* I was stepping into instead of just telling me to go away like some dumb tourist—"

"You know who Pele is?" Polunu said, cutting him off, his brown eyes wide with curiosity. "She is *akua,* cuz. That's what you're stepping into. And you ain't ready for nothing like it."

"*Akua*?" Gray asked, wrinkling his brow. "What's that?"

Polunu sighed. "It's trouble," he said. He picked up the machete and started digging around in the tabletop with its point, scratching haphazard lines into the wood. "You think you're looking for a woman? Nah, braddah. Pele ain't a woman."

Gray frowned. "What is she, then?"

"Pele is powerful; Pele is strong. Pele is a whole other level, braddah." Polunu leaned in close and whispered, "Because Pele is a *god.*"

# Chapter 6

"So when you say 'god,' you mean...?"

"I mean *god*, braddah." Polunu popped a piece of pineapple into his mouth and swallowed it without chewing. Juice dribbled down his chin, and he wiped it on his shirt, exposing his great belly, round and tight as a drum. "Larger-than-life, stronger-than-strong, start-fights-that-cause-earthquakes-and-kill-mortals-and-leave-behind-canyons *god*."

Gray wrinkled his brow. "Like...a Zeus-Aphrodite-Olympus-style *god*?"

Polunu considered this. "Yeah. Sort of like them. But with a better tan."

"That's insane." Gray passed a hand over his forehead and realized he was covered in a thick sheen of sweat, even though it wasn't really all that hot out. Also, his heart was pounding, and he felt a little dizzy.

"Insane, maybe, but that don't make it wrong," Polunu insisted.

"Oh, come on," Gray said, laughing harshly, a sound totally unrecognizable to his own ears. "Are you being serious right now?"

"Serious as a daydream."

"You actually think that *mythological Hawai'ian gods* are *real*?" He spread his arms wide, gesturing toward the old wooden table and the broken-down Volkswagen. "And *here*?"

"What, you think it's normal that crabs go around writing secret messages in the sand all the time?" Polunu laughed. "In cursive? Who you think would even teach them cursive? That's like a dead language."

"I don't know how to explain the crabs," Gray admitted, sitting down hard on the bench opposite the Hawai'ian. He put his forehead in his hands. "I'm trying not to think about it."

Polunu grunted happily and chomped down on another piece of pineapple. "You better *start* thinking about it," he said with his mouth full. "It's only gonna get weirder from here."

"Okay. Hold on." Gray scrubbed his hands against his face, hard, hoping that when he opened his eyes again, he'd be back in the hotel, maybe on the beach, waking up from some weirdly realistic rum-dream. Or maybe he was still really in St. Louis, it was the night before his wedding, Lucy hadn't left him, and none of this was real. He took a deep breath. He opened his eyes.

The big Hawai'ian's face grinned back.

"Okay. This is dumb. But whatever. Let's say gods do exist. Real, honest-to-goodness gods. Or goddesses—she'd be a god*dess*, right? Let's just say they exist. Which, for the record, I do not believe, because that's just the stupidest thing I've ever heard...but let's say they do."

"Okay," Polunu agreed, crossing his arms. "Let's say."

"Why would Hi'iaka ask me to find a mythological goddess instead of, I don't know, say, the police?"

"'Cause she's her sister."

"Who is whose sister?"

"Pele. Pele is her sister."

Gray frowned and shook his head. "Wait. Pele is *Hi'iaka's* sister?"

Polunu slapped the table. "That's right! 'Cause guess what. Your mystery girl? She is *also* a Hawai'ian goddess."

"Whoa, whoa, whoa." Gray waved his hands through the air, desperately trying to clear away the insanity. "You think *Hi'iaka* is a goddess?"

"Look, here's what I know, Grayson Park from the Mainland: I know that there's a Hi'iaka who *is* a goddess, and I know that *that* Hi'iaka is Pele's sister, and it ain't much work to figure if *your* Hi'iaka asked you to track down Pele, then it's probably *that* Pele, and *that* Hi'iaka."

Gray sliced his hands through the air like knives, punctuating his words: "But the idea of there being *ancient deities*! Alive...and *real*! There's no—it's just not—I mean, how can you even...? Polunu! It's insane!" He gasped. "Oh no. Polunu. *You* might be insane."

Polunu raised an eyebrow. "You don't believe in gods?"

"I don't believe in a *pantheon*!"

Polunu was silent as he thought about this. He offered the last piece of pineapple to Gray, who just shook his head. So he shrugged and popped it in his mouth. "You know what I think?" he said finally.

Gray sighed. "What?"

"I think the gods are all around us, always, but you gotta know where to look."

"How wonderfully philosophic." Gray shook his head. He stood up from the bench and began pacing on the far side of the table. "Look," he said, his voice softer, "mythology is called mythology because the stories are *myths*—fictions that helped ancient people make sense of a world they didn't fully understand. We don't live in a world where a group of anthropomorphic super-creatures descended from their thrones on the mountaintops to create the earth so they could have a world-sized playground."

Polunu raised a finger the size of a billy club. "Our gods don't come from mountains," he said. "They come from Tahiti."

"Well, whatever."

"I'm just trying to help."

"It doesn't matter."

"Sure it matters. Don't you know anything about mythology, brah?"

"Oh, it's worse than that," Gray said glumly. "I don't just know about it; I teach it."

Polunu gasped. "You *teach* mythology, and you don't know about the Polynesians?" he cried. His face fell, and he shook his head sadly. "Oh, Grayson Park..."

"I only get one week to cover the whole unit!" he cried, coming admirably to his own defense.

"That's sad, cuz. That makes me so sad."

"Well, don't cry, please. You'll flood the whole jungle. I'm just saying that maybe there's a God, or some higher-power *something*, but I don't believe it's Zeus and the Greeks, or Jupiter and the Romans, or Odin and the Norse, or Ra and the Egyptians, and I *definitely* don't believe it's Pele and the Polynesians."

Polunu let his chin droop to his chest, and for a second Gray thought the big man actually *might* cry. But after a few moments of silence, he lifted his head and smiled. "It's like narwhals," he said.

Gray blinked. "Narwhals?"

"Yeah. Narwhals. You know...like unicorn dolphins."

"Yeah. I know. What about them?"

"Do you know they really exist?"

"I don't know. Yeah…I guess." Gray suddenly felt annoyed, though he couldn't quite pin down why. "I mean, I don't sit around and contemplate the great and powerful narwhal, but I know they exist. So what?"

"Lots of people think they *don't* exist, 'cause they look so strange, you know? Little spiral horn and all." He held his hand up to his forehead and thrust his finger up into the air. He even gave it a little swirl for effect. "Weird, right?"

"Yeah. Pretty weird."

"It's not *pretty* weird; it's *weird as hell*, brah. People see that, and they think, 'Whoa! That can't possibly be real.' They never seen anything like it before, so they can't understand it. You know?"

"Okay," Gray said, planting his hands on his hips. "So what?"

"So lots of people think the narwhal is just a myth. Like the gods. But just because you don't understand something and ain't never seen it yourself, that don't mean it ain't real." He tapped the side of his head. "Sometimes, you only know the things you know."

Gray scratched his jaw. He slapped at a mosquito that buzzed up against his neck. What the hell was he doing out here, on the side of a road on the edge of a rainforest, talking about ancient gods with an 800-pound Hawai'ian selling fruit from a burned-out van? Whose life was he living right now? *This is all Lucy's fault*, he thought, watching the cars roll past along the highway. *She put me here, and I hope she dies alone.*

He wondered what it would feel like to mean it.

He turned and looked back at Polunu. It was pretty clear the man was either on some pretty serious medication, or he needed to be. Prehistoric gods running around in the twenty-first century…it was so far beyond nonsense that it couldn't even register. Still, Gray couldn't explain the behavior of the sand crabs, or the message they'd left him on the beach. And there *was* something otherworldly about Hi'iaka, wasn't there? Not just in her unearthly beauty, but in the way she seemed to glow, from the inside, from her spirit. It was as if she radiated divinity.

And when she touched Gray, he felt that tingling warmth.

Whatever she was, she wasn't like any human Gray had ever met before. And he couldn't explain that, either.

*But I guess sometimes you only know the things you know,* he thought.

He took a deep breath, then let it out. "All right. So you think a whole host of Hawai'ian gods *really* exist?"

Polunu smiled and shrugged. "Who knows? Maybe not. Maybe you got it right. Maybe your girl ain't no *akua,* and your hotel got some seriously messed up crab infestation on its hands. If that's the case, you're all good. You just go to the police, and they take it from here. But I tell you, if she *is* a goddess, and you go down the Pele path...braddah, you gotta be ready for what's next."

All the moisture evaporated from Gray's mouth. "What's next?" he asked uneasily.

Polunu snorted. "Pele will mean *business,* cuz. It ain't no small thing to confront a goddess, but *especially* one like Pele. She got a fiery temper, you know? You want to deliver her the message, you better be sure you can handle the heat."

"I can deliver a message," Gray said, feeling reasonably sure it was true. "It's just words. I can say words."

"You every try saying words to a raging fire?"

Gray thought about that. "Well...no," he said.

"The fire don't like to listen. The fire likes to *burn.* You keep it in mind."

"Got it," Gray said miserably, feeling prickles against his skin. He shivered. "Thanks."

"No problem!" Polunu said, nodding happily. "And hey, if you *do* want to go down that road, you really came to the right place."

"Why's that?" Gray said glumly.

"'Cause I know all about the gods," he said proudly, tapping his temple. "And I think I can help you find Pele."

Gray snorted. "Oh yeah? You guys hang out on your days off?"

"Nah. But Hawai'ian legend is strong in my family. It's strong in here," he said, fluttering his hand against his chest. "I feel *nā akua* in my heart. I think I know where you should look. If you wanna cross that line."

Gray shook his head again and pressed the heels of his hands to his cheeks. "This is so stupid," he muttered to himself.

"So what you think, *haole*? What you gonna do?"

"I don't know," Gray admitted. "What do *you* think I should do?"

"Oh no, brah. This is your decision. I'm just a guide along for the ride."

"Well, do you think it's a good idea? Or a bad idea?"

"Oh, I think it's a *terrible* idea. Why you wanna mess with the gods? They don't play by our rules, cuz. They play hard, and they play *mean*, and their games don't *have* rules."

"So you wouldn't do it."

Polunu thought about that. "Hmm…" he said as he rubbed his chins. "Well…if a pretty girl tells me some masked man is hunting her down in her dreams, then she disappears, sends me a message with crabs in cursive, asking me for help? Yeah, cuz…I guess I'd do what I can to help that pretty girl out. *Akua* or no, I think I ain't much good if I can't help other people on this earth, you know? Even if the problem is impossible."

Gray exhaled slowly, his breath rattling through his teeth. "Yeah," he said. "Even if the problem is impossible. That's pretty much what I think, too."

"Plus, what you got to lose? You don't even believe in the gods. You can't be scared of something you think don't exist."

"I guess that's true, too."

Polunu grinned. "So we going on an adventure?" he asked.

"Sure. Why not? Might as well see how far this train can go, right?" Gray extended his hand toward the Hawai'ian.

Polunu frowned down at it. "What's that?"

Gray tilted his head. "It's a hand."

"I know it's a hand," Polunu said suspiciously. "What's it doing?"

"What do you mean, what's it doing? It's waiting for you to shake it."

"Why?"

"I don't know. It just seemed like...we're starting something big together, we should shake hands."

"Nah." Polunu grinned his huge grin and lumbered around the table. "We're into the stuff of *legends*, brah—you're my *cousin* now! Cousins don't shake hands; cousins *hug*!" He threw his arms around Gray and squeezed. Gray tried to scream out in pain, but his lungs were crushed beneath Polunu's flabby, powerful arms, and his mouth was buried in the big man's belly. Polunu swatted him on the back, and Gray's teeth clacked together. He tried to pat his new friend in return, but his arms were pinned, so he just flailed his hands like dying fish until Polunu was satisfied.

When the big man pulled away, there were tears glistening in his eyes. "This is a beautiful thing," he said. "But, you know, before we get started, I gotta tell you something," he said, boxing up the fruit and tossing it into the van.

"What's that?" Gray asked, pulling new air into his re-inflating lungs.

Polunu closed the door and clapped the dirt from his hands. "Pele doesn't mess around for *real*, cuz. And if we do find her, there's a pretty good chance that she'll just kill you for fun."

# Chapter 7

"*Why didn't* you *drive?!*" Gray screamed.

He hadn't meant to scream. But his hands were cemented to the wheel; his spine burned from sitting so erect, his eyes blurred from focusing so hard on the road, and he had never been so terrified while moving so slowly in his entire life. He screamed because his biology gave him no other choice.

"I don't like to drive," Polunu said, shifting his bulk in the passenger seat. "You miss too much of the scenery that way."

Watching that mountain of a man squeeze into the little Corolla was like watching someone stuff a sausage into a Tic-Tac container. He filled the cabin like an over-inflated life raft, and his inadvertent crowding added claustrophobia to Gray's current—and growing—list of fears. "I hope you enjoy the scenery when we're *dead!*"

Gray ground his teeth into powder as he piloted them slowly along the Road to Hana, an interminable snake of a two-lane road that wound like a coiled rope through the cliffs and forests of Maui's northeastern coast. The road doubled back on itself every few hundred feet with a series of razor-sharp U-bends, and each one sent Gray's stomach into spasms. The outside curves hovered the cars a thousand feet over the crashing ocean; the interior curves squeezed them along one-lane bridges with surging waterfalls on one side and bottomless gullies on the other. To top it all off, it was raining, and even with the windshield wipers scratching frantically against the onslaught, sheets of water still cascaded across the glass, and every single thing in Gray's vision was blurred into shapeless doubles. "I can't do it!" he screeched, jerking the wheel to the right as an oncoming Jeep whipped around the curve with its tires over the yellow line. "*I can't do it!*"

"Relax, brah; you doing good," Polunu assured him, smiling out the passenger window and waving to a carful of trembling tourists who had pulled over to the side of the road to take a breath. "Besides, you think the Road to Hana is bad, you should see it when you get *past* Hana! Unpaved, washed out, just one lane of two-way traffic, no guardrails, heavy wind. And goats, too. Lots of goats."

"Goats?" Gray said, swallowing down the urge to puke as they snailed across a bridge that spanned a deep, open canyon.

Polunu nodded. "Goats, braddah. They *own* that road. One wrong move on the other side—woooo! You slip out over 4,000 feet of ocean air. This road? Paved, guardrails...this road is *nice*. This is the *tourist* road."

"I'll remember that when we're upside-down in a ditch," Gray mumbled. He glanced at the clock. The day had crossed into the early afternoon. "How much farther?" he asked.

"Not too far," Polunu assured him. "Maybe 20 more miles or something."

Gray gaped down at the speedometer. "I can't do this road for another hour," he whispered, his voice hoarse from the screaming.

Polunu shrugged. "Just go faster then," he smiled. "That makes it quicker."

"Shut up."

They drove on in silence, Gray's knuckles glowing white from the strain of controlling the wheel. Every few minutes, another car would roar up onto his tail, and Gray would risk one hand off the wheel to throw it out the window and wave the person frantically around. He could get there fast, or he could get there alive, but he was pretty sure he couldn't do both.

He had never been so tense or uncomfortable in his life.

Or so miserable.

"Ooo, Coconut Glen's!" Polunu cheered, stubbing his finger against the window and pointing to a little shack on the side of the road. "Pull over!"

"I *can't* pull over!" Gray screamed.

"But coconut ice cream, cuz! *Coconut ice cream!*"

Gray gritted his teeth. He checked his mirrors.

Then he pulled over for coconut ice cream.

An hour later, they rolled into the lot that fronted the entrance to the cave. "We made it," Polunu said with a grin. He gave Gray a nudge that sent the smaller man smashing against the driver-side door. "Safe and sound, yeah?" He popped open his door and heaved himself out of the car. The Corolla rocked like a ship in a wake.

"Yeah," Gray whispered to the empty cabin. "Safe. Safe and... and sound."

It took him a full thirty seconds to peel his fingers from the wheel.

They stood together at the mouth of the cave. Gray frowned. "This is where Pele lives?" he asked. It was little more than a glorified hole in the ground. He was starting to suspect that Pele might be less of a goddess and more of a raving-mad homeless woman, squatting in a national park.

"Not exactly. This is how we *get* to Pele's home," Polunu corrected him. "Maybe. If what my heart tells me is true."

Gray shook his head in disbelief. "It looks like a tourist trap. The kind where you get rolled for your Clif bars and left for dead," he said. As if on cue, a pair of hikers climbed out of the cave, laughing and shaking the dirt from their hands.

"Oh, yeah, it's definitely that, too," Polunu agreed. He raised his fist and stuck out his thumb and his pinky. He waved the *shaka* at the pair of hikers. "*Aloha*, cousins!" he cried.

The hikers waved back. One of them tried to make a *shaka* with his own hand, but ended up throwing metal horns instead. He shrugged and went with it. "*Aloha!*" they cheered.

Gray raised an eyebrow at his guide. "You're a happy sort of person, aren't you?"

"What's not to be happy about? The sky is blue, the grass is green, and the ocean is a gift that never ceases to give."

"Yeah, but it rains a lot, too," Gray grumbled.

"We have a saying in Hawai'i," Polunu began.

Gray shook his head. "Of course you do."

"We say, 'Rain makes the taro grow.'"

"In Missouri, we say, 'Rain, rain, go away, come again some other day.'"

"Oh, so it's *all* Missourians who are grumpy," Polunu said, giving Gray another nudge. He smiled broadly. "Come on, *haole*. Let's go get a beat on your girl. Maybe she can lighten you up."

Gray couldn't argue with that. So he shrugged and followed Polunu into the cave.

"This is a lava tube," the Hawai'ian explained as they climbed over the rough, knobby rock. "Long time ago, you take this walk, you get all red and melty. You ever time-travel a million years to the past, don't you come back down here, cuz."

"Thanks for the tip."

They hobbled slowly along, guided by the dim light that filtered in through natural skylights in the ceiling of the cave. It wasn't a deep tunnel, and after about five minutes of walking they reached the limit of the cave, a spot where the rock overhead opened up into a huge, broad circle. A shaft of sunlight thrust itself down to the cave floor, casting a surreal glow in the underground place. A handful of other visitors sat within the light, half a dozen teenagers sunbathing fifty feet below the surface of the Earth.

"*Aloha!*" Polunu said.

"*Aloha!*" they all replied.

"*Aloha,*" Gray added, but it sounded way too forced, like when upper-middle class white people walk into a Mexican bakery and say, "*Hola,*" so he vowed to probably never say it again.

"You guys having a good time? Enjoying the lava?"

The kids murmured happily in response.

"Good, good. You ever go back in time a million years, though, don't come *here*!" They laughed.

Gray gave Polunu a look.

"What?" he asked, shrugging his big shoulders. "It's new to them."

"Is one of *them* Pele?" Gray whispered, rolling his eyes. "That one looks like the stuff of gods." He pointed to a girl who was attempting a handstand on the floor of the cave. She kicked her feet up into the air, then quickly lost balance. Her hands flew out from beneath her, and she crashed back down on her face. The other kids laughed.

Polunu slapped Gray on the back. "You gotta have faith, bradd-ah. Your whole attitude, you know? Trust me. It's about to change." He pulled Gray back down the cave a little ways toward the entrance, until he found a section where the floor was smooth. "Here. This looks like a good spot, yeah?"

Gray groaned in frustration. "A good spot for *what*?"

"For giving you a whole new outlook." Polunu grinned and knelt down on the floor and motioned for Gray to do the same. He did, reluctantly, balancing his knees on the hard, porous stone. "Pele is the goddess of fire and volcanoes. This lava tube, it falls under her domain, you know? This ground..." Polunu patted the ground beneath them. "This is Pele's place. Put your hand here. Rest your palm there. Yeah, like that. You feel it? You feel the *depth* of this place?"

Gray's tongue poked out of the corner of his mouth as he concentrated on his hand. "I feel...*something*," he admitted, though the thing he felt most was a sharp, painful corner of stone.

"That's good," Polunu nodded. "You touch this stone, you're connected to Pele. To her history, and her power. That's important."

"Okay," Gray conceded. "I get it. Pele rules volcanoes; so get close to a volcano, and you get close to Pele. Great. Do we just...ask the rock?"

Polunu screwed up his mouth in confusion. "Ask it what?"

"You know. To go save Hi'iaka."

Polunu scratched the knot of hair on top of his head. "Why would we do that?"

"Because it's Pele!" Gray said. His voice echoed down to the sunbathing kids. They turned to stare. He gave them a dismissive wave. "Because it's Pele," he said again, more quietly. "You said—"

"I said this is *connected* to Pele, not that it *is* Pele. Dang, *haole*, I don't want to sign up for this trouble with someone who talks to rocks."

"All right, all right, shut up," Gray grumbled. Polunu laughed. "Then...what do we do? How do we *get* to Pele?"

"Ah! Now you're asking the right question," Polunu said, tapping his temple. "First, we need *hoʻokupu*."

"*Hoʻokupu*?"

"It's like a gift, you know? We present Pele with a gift, and see if she opens the door."

"Oh! Hey, I know this one!" Gray said, brightening a bit. "The concierge this morning, she told me if I was going to find Pele, I should bring her some gin."

"Puh!" Polunu said. He made an angry gesture with his fingers. "Gin. That concierge must have been a real *haole*."

"All right, you keep saying '*haole*.' What does that mean?"

"It means like a stupid white person from the mainland."

"What?!"

Polunu shrugged. "You asked."

"You've called me that, like, a hundred times!"

"Yeah, you're *haole*, but you're, like, a *good haole*. You know?"

"No," Gray said, narrowing his eyes and crossing his arms. "I *don't* know."

Polunu grinned. "A nice *haole* is still *haole*. But you're a good person, Grayson Park. You're crabby today, but I see your soul." He reached out and patted Gray's heart. "You doing a big thing right now for the right reasons. You're a good man. You're a good *haole*. It's like a compliment. But a bad *haole*...that's someone who comes from the mainland and gets all white over the Hawai'ian culture. You know? Like people who come to the beach and steal sea glass. That's *our* sea glass, cuz. You know? Don't take that sea glass. That's *our* sea glass."

"You're a big fan of sea glass," Gray observed.

"It's beautiful," Polunu nodded. "Just an example, you know. But I do like it."

"So I'm a good *haole* and the concierge is a bad *haole*."

"That's right."

"Because she likes gin."

"No, no, no. Because she thinks *Pele* likes gin. That's a white people's rumor. Why would Pele drink gin? If she's gonna do shots, she'll do, like, rum or something. With Hawai'ian sugarcane. Keep it local."

"Okay. So did you bring any rum?"

Polunu burst out laughing. "Rum? Pele don't drink rum! Damn, cuz, don't be such a bad *haole*."

Gray rubbed his temples to show his deep and undying annoyance, but he couldn't help but laugh. "I hate you," he said. "Just so you know."

Polunu grinned. "I love you too, cuz. I love you too."

"All right. So if she doesn't like gin and she doesn't like rum, what *does* she like?"

Polunu rubbed his hands together excitedly. "A good *ho'okupu* is all about intention. You gotta give a *ho'okupu* with something *real* behind it."

"I hope we can put something real behind a five-dollar bill," Gray said, patting his pockets, "'cause that's about all I got."

"Sometimes just the intention is enough," Polunu said, closing his eyes. "You keep the money, but share your positive vibes." He took deep breaths and placed his hands tenderly on the sloping wall before them. His lips moved imperceptibly with the words of his intention. Then he opened one eye and peered over at his companion. He cleared his throat. "Okay, mainlander. Anytime."

"Oh. Sorry." Gray mimicked his guide, closing his eyes and laying his hands against the stone. He thought about Hi'iaka, about the wind chimes in her laugh and her vanilla-salt scent. He remembered the quiet plea in her coffee-brown eyes when she spoke to him of her dreams, and he felt the warmth of her touch on his wrist, the heat that unrolled like a blanket across his arm.

His own lips moved, and he whispered to the stone: "I'll find Pele for you, Hi'iaka. I promise. She'll find you, she'll bring you back, and I will see you again."

The warmth on his arm became real, and now it spread down to his wrist, pooling across his palm, melting against the tips of his fingers. His hand pulsed with the heat...and then the sensation grew, warming his skin, tingling his flesh, until it was hot—*burning* hot, and suddenly, his palm was on fire. He yanked his hand back from the stone, crying out in pain. He opened his eyes, and his jaw dropped. The cave wall before him that was cold and black only seconds ago was now glowing red with heat.

"You gotta let go when things turn to lava, cuz," Polunu chided, clicking his tongue in disappointment. "Don't you know nothing?"

"What is—?" Gray began, but he couldn't finish the thought. Before his eyes, the red glow of the wall spread wider and wider, creeping outward from the place where their hands had pressed against the stone. Then the center intensified to a brilliant orange-white, and the bright, hot stone began to drip down the wall, melting into trickles of lava that snaked lazily down the cave wall. Gray leapt to his feet and took a few steps back as the wall continued to dissolve into a pool that cooled down to a dark red-orange as it spread across the cave floor. Soon, the whole wide circle of stone had melted away, leaving a gaping hole in the wall.

Gray gasped.

Polunu nodded. "You got good intention, brah," he said, giving Gray a bit of a sideways hug. "I knew it. You're a good *haole*."

"That...is...impossible," Gray said, digging for words like they were suspended in Jell-O. The puddle of lava at their feet had already cooled back down to a solid mass of rock, and Gray leaned closer, peering through the newly-formed hole in the wall. In the dim light, he could just barely make out a lava-rock staircase descending down, down, down into the darkness on the other side. "Are you *seeing* this?" he hissed, completely unable to take a full breath.

"I see it," Polunu nodded. "I guess Pele wants to talk to you, too."

Gray spun toward the group of teenagers for further confirmation, but they just sat in their sunbeam, blinking and chatting and completely nonplussed.

"Do they not see this?" he demanded. "Is this not impressive enough? My God, what is wrong with Millennials?!"

But Polunu shook his head. "They don't see, brah. They don't have the right intention."

"This is just..." Gray stopped, and he shrugged, shaking his head with his mouth agape. "I don't know. There's no word for what this is."

"That's the truth," the Hawai'ian agreed. Then he gestured toward the hole in the wall. "After you."

Gray stepped nervously through the opening and tested the top step with the toe of his sandal. His skin didn't melt off on contact, which he took as a pretty good sign. He put his whole weight on the stair, and it didn't crumble away. "That's encouraging." He peered down the staircase and squinted into the darkness below. Then he cursed.

"What?" Polunu asked excitedly. "What do you see?"

"Nothing. That's the problem. It's dark as hell down—" But before he could finish, the edges of the steps began warming to a gentle glow, starting at the top where he stood and slowly working downward until the entire staircase was outlined in thin, orange ribbons of molten rock. "Ooookay," Gray said, taking a deep breath. "Now *that's* happening."

"I'm glad you're going first," Polunu confided.

"Thanks. Thanks a lot."

Gray stepped down the staircase, careful to plant his feet gingerly in the center of each step, avoiding the cracks of lava that shone through along the edges. He stepped as lightly as he could, but every few steps he pressed too hard, and a stream of molten magma would squirt through the openings, splashing and hissing onto the stone stair and down into the abyss on either side.

Polunu had a more difficult time. Each foot was the weight of a boulder, which made the lava beneath him stream up and spill around his sandals at every stair. "Next time, remind me to wear shoes," he said miserably. He concentrated hard on bringing his foot down in the very center of each step, where the lava had a harder time reaching him.

Down they crept, following the glowing orange lines as the steps curved to the right, then to the left, then back to the right, and back around to the left. The staircase spun and swirled, spiraling deeper and deeper into the earth. At one point, the grade broke into a flat walkway, and after a dozen yards, the steps reappeared, leading upward this time. They wound in every conceivable direction, and as the two men followed the path, time crawled, and slowed, and stretched, until Gray couldn't tell what day it was, or what week, or what year. "How long have we been walking?" he whispered over his shoulder, because anything louder felt like it might bring the whole cave down on their heads.

"No tellin', cuz. We've crossed over."

Gray halted, and Polunu slammed into him from behind. Gray cried out and tumbled down six steps, hands first, narrowly avoiding eighth-degree burns and a plunge over the edge into darkness. "Hey!"

"Whoops...sorry," Polunu said. He peered into the darkness. "You still alive down there?"

"Barely." Gray lifted himself carefully to his feet, balancing uneasily on the precarious step. "What do you mean, we've 'crossed over?'"

"Into the realm of the gods, you know? Time don't work for them like it works for us. Maybe we been down here a long time; maybe we hardly been down here at all." He eased himself down closer to Gray's step and gave him a little nudge. "Best not to think about it. And just keep going."

"Sure," Gray murmured, taking a breath and resuming his descent. "Don't think about it, and just keep going. What could go wrong?"

But soon Gray's foot hit the bottom step. A new walkway opened up, and the lava outline spread far ahead of him, illuminating a wide, circular platform. It butted up against another rock wall, which was solid except for a rough rectangular hole that opened to the other side. Flames flickered within the next room, throwing long, wicked shadows across the platform that licked hungrily at the men's feet.

Gray looked at Polunu. Polunu looked at Gray.

"You go first," they said at the same time.

"No way, brah," Polunu said, raising his hands defensively and backing up toward the steps. "This is your quest."

"But you're the expert!" Gray hissed.

"And the expert says that you should go first."

"That is so unfair!"

"I won't even fit through that hole!"

"Let's find out!"

"No way!"

"Did you come this far to bicker over who gets incinerated first?"

Both men froze as a third voice rang through the vast cavern, resounding across the rocks. It was a woman's voice, more authoritative and rich than any Gray had ever heard before. It blazed with annoyance and set the air crackling with impatience.

"Ooooh...you made her mad," Polunu whispered, giving Gray a hard shove toward the door. "Go now. Or we're both dead."

Under the circumstances, it was pretty hard to argue.

Gray stepped through the opening, his whole body trembling with fear. He gripped the far end of the shallow tunnel and slowly pulled himself through, peeking around the edge at the wide room beyond.

The chamber was circular, with a pit of roiling, sputtering lava spilling up onto the ledge of the floor. Parts of the stone underfoot were little more than a fragile, crackling black skin that floated atop the tremulous magma, breaking here and oozing there, sinking beneath the pool only to rise again with glowing orange fingers spreading lazily across the surface. The air was a boiling mist; after only a few seconds, Gray had soaked through his t-shirt. Streams of sweat poured down his cheeks, and a small puddle began to spread around his feet. The light of the lava flow was brilliant, and Gray raised a hand to shield his eyes, but there were already blue-yellow streaks slashing across his vision when he closed his eyes.

And each time he dared to open them, he saw the woman standing in the center of the cauldron, tall and proud and ankle-deep in the viscous, boiling flames.

She towered over him, leering down from the ceiling of the conical chamber. She was striking, beautiful even, and unlike anything else on earth. Her long hair was the shimmering black of polished rock at the roots, but as it cascaded across her shoulders and down her chest and back, it gradually brightened to a brilliant orange-white, and the tips dripped teardrops of fire down into the lava pit in which she stood. Her skin was dark, almost black, and like the cooling skin of the magma, it was split with thin fingers of reddish-orange light, where the lava churned beneath the surface and threatened to burst through and dribble down her arms, her legs, her shoulders, and her chest. She wore a close-fitting shift like dark ash smeared across her body, with tiny cinder-flakes smoldering and smoking in the heat.

"What business have you here?" she asked angrily. The lava bubbled higher, boiling up to her knees before calming back down into the pit.

Gray opened his mouth to speak, but his voice refused to co-operate. So he stood there, open-mouthed and silent, staring at the enormous woman made of liquid fire, until Polunu squirmed through the opening and prodded him to the side.

The big man gasped. "Pele," he breathed, stunned by her presence. He fell clumsily to his knees despite the oppressive heat and lowered his chest to the floor of the cavern, lying prostrate before the churning lava.

Gray only stood and gaped.

"Psst," Polunu said, tilting his head and eyeing Gray from the side. He waved his hand frantically.

"What?" Gray whispered.

Polunu waved even harder.

The meaning was completely lost on the mainlander. "What?!" he whispered again, more harshly.

"Get on the ground!" Polunu hissed back.

"There's lava down there!"

"There's a goddess up *there*!"

"So?!"

"*So*? So show her respect, you dumb *haole*!"

Grayson gasped. "I *knew* you thought I was dumb!"

"Enough." The woman's voice singed the air. Her breath smelled of ozone and sulfur. "Say what you have come to say." Her eyes were pools of burning oil, and they flared with anger.

"You...you're Pele?" Gray asked.

"You've come a long way to ask insufferable questions," the woman spat. The temperature of the room increased by an easy five degrees, and Gray could feel the moisture evaporating from his skin.

"I'm sorry," he cried, shrinking back against the tunnel as his thoughts mashed together in his brain like a heat fever. "I don't mean to be insufferable. I'm from St. Louis."

Polunu swatted back with his hand and smacked Gray's ankle.

Gray screeched in pain. "I'm sorry!" he wailed. "I just can't—it's not—I'm just so *hot!*"

The crackling light beneath Pele's skin softened, and she drew back from the edge of the cauldron. The heat faded with her, and Gray felt the burn on his skin die down to a low, throbbing pulse. "I'm sorry," he said again, his chest heaving, his lungs pulling in hot, stifling breaths. "I just...I have a message for you. From...Hi'iaka."

Pele grew still in her fiery pool. Her fingers tensed, and her back stiffened. "What does my sister say?" she asked, her voice trembling with a boiling undercurrent.

"What does she say? Um, well, basically, she—"

"What *exactly* does she say?" Pele hissed. The lava seemed to push her up, make her even taller, until the crown of her head scraped the top of the cavern.

Gray trembled so hard, his teeth rattled in his skull. "Exactly? Oh. Okay. Um. She said...she said..." He closed his eyes and tried to picture the crabs' cursive words in the sand, but the heat and the sweat and the threat of divine incineration seemed to muddle the image.

Polunu heaved himself to his feet and edged backward, closer to Gray. He whispered out of the side of his mouth, "Tell her what she said, cuz."

"I'm thinking!" he hissed back. "Okay. She said...'Captured by the man in black.' Wait, no. 'Captured by the man...in the black hood. Help me, Grayson. Find Pele.'"

The volcano goddess melted into herself, becoming a woman-shaped glob of lava. She sank slowly into the cauldron, and the level of the magma rose. Gray and Polunu both retreated, pressing themselves as flat against the wall as they could, and the lava washed up within inches of their toes. The rubber on Gray's flip-flops began to smoke. "Please! I'm telling the truth, that's what she said!" he screamed.

The lava began to reform itself, and Pele reemerged smaller, standing at eye level. She stepped out of the fiery pool and approached the pair, addressing Gray directly. "Who are you, mainlander?" she demanded. Her tongue was a porous stone that danced with flame. "Why did you let her be taken?"

"I'm nobody," he insisted. "I'm a tourist." His heart beat so rapidly, he clutched his chest. *I'm having a heart attack,* he thought. Pele's eyes flared, but she did not interrupt. "I—I didn't let her be taken...I promise. I don't even know her, not really. We met last night, and she left, and then she sent me a message, with the crabs, and the sand, and...please, oh god...please, *please* don't melt me."

"Why would Hi'iaka present herself to *you*?" Pele seethed.

"I don't know! I don't know, I don't know!" He wailed "I don't want to be a volcano!"

Polunu took a small step forward and cleared his throat. "*Tūtū* Pele," he said, finding his voice, and spreading his hands wide in a show of surrender, "we are blessed by your presence. This *haole* does not know the old ways. Hi'iaka-i-ka-poli-o-Pele surely chose him to deliver her message for good reason, and I think his heart is pure. He's not so smart about some things, but look into his eyes. I think you'll see goodness there." Polunu gave Gray a sideways glance. "Behind all the tears. He doesn't usually cry so much."

"I don't!" Gray insisted.

Pele stepped even closer, and Gray fought with every fiber of his being to not shrink away from her blazing stare. He locked eyes with the fire goddess, and he was only semi-conscious of the feeling of wet warmth spreading across the front of his shorts.

But the great Polynesian deity was sated by what she saw behind Gray's tears, and she stepped back to her lava pool, clasping her hands behind her back. "Did my sweet sister say nothing more?" she asked, her voice softer.

"She—she said the man in the black veil was chasing her in her dreams, and she was running from him..."

"Tell her about the moon," Polunu whispered.

"Oh! The moon! She was running toward the moon. She thought he would stop chasing her when the moon was full."

"The full moon..." Pele said, mostly to herself.

"*La luna,*" Gray added weakly. He closed his eyes and shook his head and cursed himself for saying so many dumb, senseless things in such a short amount of time.

Pele floated in her bubbling lake, bobbing thoughtfully along the surface. "The moon comes full tomorrow night," she said at last, her hand trailing in the lava as it swirled around her feet. "You must find her before then."

Gray gasped and inhaled a breath of sulfur and hot ash. He choked and gagged, coughing himself inside out. "*I* must find her before then?!"

"The both of you."

"But—" Gray looked at Polunu. The big man's eyes were wide with fear. He gave his great head a shake that made his cheeks wobble. Gray turned back to the goddess. "I don't...we thought...I'm not..."

"Say what you will say," Pele commanded.

"It's just...we thought maybe...we would just deliver the message, and...*you* would find her?"

Polunu nodded his agreement.

Pele continued to swirl the fire. "My sister revealed herself to you because she knows I cannot interfere; it falls on you to come to her aid."

"*Tūtū* Pele," Polunu said, shooting a nervous glance at Gray, "we are not really equipped for that sort of task, you know?"

"You are not," Pele agreed. She brought her other hand down into the lava and began turning complex patterns in the orange goo. "But I cannot leave this place. My wicked sister, the wild and vengeful goddess Nāmaka, has extinguished all of my volcanoes, save this one. Were I to leave it unattended, she would surely douse its fires, and thereby my own flame as well. I cannot allow this...there is so much work yet to be done." She reached her hands down into the lava and pulled up a large formation of black rock. "Even now, I am creating a new island for my Hawai'i," she said softly, running her fingertips tenderly along the cliffs and valleys. "Lō'ihi will nurture my people for eons to come. It will be fierce and beautiful, and it will remind my Hawai'ians of their raw and wild history." She set the miniature island on the surface of the lava carefully, and it slowly melted away, becoming one with the burning pool. "I cannot go to save my sweet sister, for the evil one will seize her opportunity when it comes. I must stay, not only for my own survival, but for the survival of my people, of my beloved Hawai'i." She gazed down at little Lō'ihi until it sank fully beneath the surface. She wept a tear of fire that sizzled against her skin as she wiped it from her cheek with a blackened, burning hand. She looked up at her guests, blinking at them in wonder, as if she'd forgotten they existed altogether. Then the hardness returned to her voice, and the flame rekindled in her eyes. "You must find her. You must set her free before midnight tomorrow. If you fail, your agony will be beyond measure."

Grayson bit his bottom lip. "Miss Pele, ma'am, I'm just really not sure—"

She moved like an explosion, and the air thundered with the wavering heat of steam and ash. She swooped up against the lip of the cauldron, splashing lava onto the floor once again. A small wave crashed at Gray's feet, and a bubble of magma burst as the wave fell. It flung fiery droplets against Gray's shoulder, and he screamed in pain. The lava seared through his shirt and into his flesh, bubbling his skin. Then Pele blew a cold wind across the cavern, and the lava immediately cooled to pellets of rock. The bits dropped out of Gray's shoulder, and the pain faded to a cool numbness. He clutched his shoulder, whimpering and drawing deep, stuttering breaths of shock and fear. "You...*burned* me," he gasped.

Polunu clapped a hand over his own mouth. He ran out of the room so he wouldn't throw up in the presence of a goddess.

"Do not fail," Pele repeated. "I will not tolerate losing my sweet sister because of your weakness."

"We'll...try," Gray said, wiping the tears and sweat from his face as he backed toward the door. "Okay? We'll...we'll try."

Pele was unmoved by his fear. "Then try very, *very* hard, main-lander."

Gray eased around the cavern wall, feeling his way until his fingers found the edge of the rough doorway. "I do have *one* question..." he said.

Pele's fire roared, and her hair flared around her like an inferno.

"Please don't burn me! Please don't burn me! I mean this with *total* respect, please, but...*how* do we find her?"

He squeezed his eyes shut and waited for another wave of fire. But Pele's eyes cooled instead, hardening into stone. "Kamapua'a is the only creature in all of the world who is both bold enough to attack my sister and cowardly enough to hide his face while doing it. Find Kamapua'a, and you will find my Hi'iaka, my sweet and fragile egg. I suggest you try the upcountry. You will likely find him with the rest of the pigs."

"Kamapua'a," Gray said, stumbling back into the doorway. "In the upcountry. Got it. I'll just...Google him, I guess."

Polunu poked his head through the opening, pushing his face over Gray's shoulder. "*Tūtū* Pele, how can we make a stand against a terrible demigod like Kamapua'a?"

"Sorry, a *demigod*?" Gray squeaked.

"Seek Maui," Pele said, ignoring Gray's concern and sinking into the fire. "His ancient hook has the power to destroy a creature like Kamapua'a. Convince Maui to grant you the help of his hook, and you may yet survive the day."

"And if we can't?" Polunu asked.

"Then I expect you will die," Pele hissed. Her black hair spread like a stain across the glowing molten stone as her face submerged. Then she sank beneath the surface and was gone in a hiss of smoke and embers.

# Chapter 8

Hi'iaka shivered. Gooseflesh had bubbled to life all along her skin.

But she wasn't cold. And she wasn't scared.

She was furious.

"Show me your face!" she screamed into the forest that lay beyond the fallen wall of the dilapidated shed. But the vicious grunting of wild pigs was her only response.

She knew what that meant.

She knew *exactly* what that meant.

It was raining outside, a brief, hard mountain storm that would pass before long. In the meantime, it dripped its cold fingers of water down on her from the rusted holes in the shack's tin ceiling. She welcomed the rain and turned her face up toward the drops, catching them on her tongue and drinking hungrily. The hard patter of the rain on the roof above and on the leaves outside calmed her, gave her something else to focus on beyond her own thoughts, and that was good.

Her own thoughts could be dangerous.

The rain beat down harder, and Hi'iaka smiled. She prayed that a flood might rise and wash her captor away. She could hear the dull roar of a river not far into the forest. She willed it to swell.

She should have fled to Moloka'i. She should have kept outrunning her dreams. But there was something about the mainlander. She wanted to see him again, and she sensed that if she had left Maui that night, their paths would not cross a second time. And she had thought that perhaps he had been right about her dreams. Maybe they had been harmless imaginings, borne of a tired heart and a complacent mind. And so she remained on Maui, her heart senselessly aflutter at the thought of her midnight rendezvous with the strange and charming Grayson Park. She combed her hair. She wore a fine blue silk. She brushed herself with lavender. She pinned a plumeria blossom in her hair. She took a deep breath and headed for the lobby.

But when she opened her door, the man from her dreams was standing there, silent as a statue, as tall and as wide as the doorframe. A black sheet covered his face and draped across his shoulders. He wore no shirt and no shoes—no clothes at all, save a pair of crude boar-skin breeches, raggedly cut and loosely fastened. Hi'iaka gasped, and that moment of surprise was all he needed. By the time she managed to react, he was inside the room, muscling his way through the door and grabbing her roughly by the shoulders. She opened her mouth to scream, and he hit her in the stomach, hard, with a closed fist. The wind left her, and she collapsed, heaving on the floor. He stood over her, his fingers flexing in anticipation. Then he removed the veil from his head and dropped it over Hi'iaka's in one fluid movement, so she never got the chance to see his face. Then he delivered another blow, this one to the side of her head, and the world exploded briefly in light, and then it fell utterly, utterly dark, and she fell with it.

She had been careless. And that had been foolish.

She should have fled to Moloka'i.

Now she was a prisoner in the upcountry, judging by the thickness of the woods, and who would dare risk the mountains to save her?

"Show me your face!" she screamed again, her voice exploding powerfully through the rain. Her hair clung in wet strings across her shoulders, and her silk dress melted to her skin. She held herself silent and waited for a response.

There was nothing but the rutting squeals of pigs.

Her prison was a flimsy shed of corrugated tin. One of the walls had fallen completely away; it was carpeted by vines and moss and wild grasses that had crept in over the years. A reddish-brown palette of rust broke through the open tangles of green.

The other three walls still stood, but just barely. One had started bowing outward; the weight of mountain rainfall would buckle it before long. The other two walls would follow, but for now, they wavered dangerously in the wind.

The roof had been patched so many times, it was little more than a metal quilt. The joints were poorly sealed, which allowed the sheet to drop water like a hard, flat rain cloud.

The upcountry forest was a dangerous and terrible place. Wild boars ruled the underbrush in the Maui hills, with their sharp, muddy tusks and their tenacious greed. But they weren't the only concern. Far from it. The land itself could kill as easily as any other wild creature, opening up in unexpected places, cracking into cliffs where there should have been dirt, dropping away to hard, cragged lava caves beneath a grove of lush and tangling trees. The rains could turn a small mountain stream into a raging torrent in a matter of minutes, sweeping a stranded goat or a foolish hiker away in its path, whipping him down the hard slopes of the mountain, crushing his bones beneath the falls, and washing his remains out into the open ocean far, far below.

But the land wasn't even the most dangerous part. The people of the upcountry followed their own primal gods, and they lived by a code kept secret to themselves. They were removed—a *hungry* people. They craved seclusion; they worshipped silence. Many stalked through the forests, armed with guns and sharpened spears, foraging through the brush, scraping out scant crops and hollowing themselves against the world.

Inside the shack was a fight for freedom. Outside the shack was a fight for survival.

Still, Hi'iaka would rather take her chances out there in the wild than be tortured here in the shed. She'd rather die on her own terms than suffer on someone else's. But if the shack was a prison, the circle carved into the mud around her feet was a cell, and she could not step beyond it, no matter how strong her will.

There were rules about these things. They were ancient, and they could not be broken.

The pigs outside the shack screamed as they gouged at each other, undaunted by the rain. Every so often, a boar rumbled over the fallen wall, skidding on the metal beneath the brush and screeching its anger. They were huge, powerful beasts, with slavering mouths and furious eyes. A few of the boars had ventured into the shack, stalking the prisoner slowly, snorting at the air, getting the scent of her. They came close to the circle, pawing at the mud and blasting her with hot air from their snouts, but they did not advance past the line.

Wild though they were, even they bowed to the primal rules.

They could not enter the circle, and she could not leave it.

Her captor had been careful to keep himself hidden, approaching the shed only at the standing walls, pressing his eye through the rust-ringed holes in the tin. He was anxious, she could tell, by the way he stalked around outside crashing through the brush and smacking the flanks of the irritable boars. Anxious for what, she couldn't say...but it had something to do with the full moon; her dreams had been clear enough on that. And the moon would be full the following night.

"*La luna*," she'd heard the mainlander say in the young hours of a morning that seemed like years ago.

She spat in the mud beyond the ring, to spread herself beyond her cell in any way she could.

She should have fled to Moloka'i.

Her captor had been stacking dry brush at the corner of the shack, half in Hi'iaka's view, half hidden by the walls. When the rain had begun to fall, he had thrown a tarp over the pile. But now, as the storm began to slow to a few spattering drops, she heard him squelching through the mud and grabbing the end of the tarp. He whisked it away with such sudden force that she jumped, to see her half of the cover ripped away. Still hidden from view, he grunted as he threw another bundle of branches on the stack. The pigs began to emerge slowly from the jungle, stepping up to the brush pile and grunting their approval. Smoke began to stream out from the bottom of the mound, first in a string of pale wisps, then a full white column, and Hi'iaka knew the man had struck fire to the kindling beneath the branches. She heard him blowing against the struggling flames, and the pigs joined in, huffing and snuffling at the fire until it caught the dry leaves at the bottom with a gentle *whoosh*. Suddenly, the brush was crackling, the whole pile lighting up with flickering flames made pale by the daylight. The boars squealed with their mad approval, and the man squealed too, screeching and stamping. The pigs whipped themselves into a frenzy, stomping over the fallen sheet of metal, smashing each other with the flats of their tusks, nipping at each other's ears, slamming each other toward the fire.

The man joined them, emerging around the edge of the fire, flinging his limbs in a mad, tribal dance, his back to his prisoner. He moved with hard, jerking steps through the sounder of boars, squealing and screeching and howling at the clouds. Then he launched himself at the pigs, grabbing them by the legs, wrestling them to the ground, shoving them about, laughing madly as they attacked him back, grunting and rolling and crashing into the fire.

The man leapt to his feet, and a boar smashed its head into his hip, causing him to turn.

In this way, he showed her his face.

It was a face she knew very well.

# Chapter 9

"How do you just *know* where to find Maui?"

The drive back from the lava tube was no less harrowing than the drive there, but Gray's mind was a little too preoccupied with his run-in with the lava-flinging volcano goddess to notice.

"Everyone knows where to find Maui," Polunu said with a shrug. "He ain't hiding, cuz."

"Oh, so *everyone* knows where to find the ancient demigod who dredged the islands up from the bottom of the ocean with his giant hook a billion years ago?"

Polunu clapped his great hands happily and smiled. "You see how much I'm teaching you about Hawai'ian mythology? You're learning the stories already!"

"Great. Good for me."

"Maui did a lot of things for Hawai'i. Not just dragging up the islands. He is, like, the all-powerful hero of Hawai'ian legend. You know. Like Hercules."

"Great. I don't care. Tell me how it's possible that he's just *hanging out* somewhere on the island for *anyone* to discover, because I've watched the news here, and he hasn't been in a single segment, and it seems like a Hawai'ian *god* might rate a cameraman or two, so I am having some pretty serious doubts."

Polunu thought about this. "I mean, people *would* know where to find him if they paid attention," he said. "He's got, like, a sign and everything."

It was well past lunchtime, and Gray felt his blood sugar falling. His eyes began to vibrate, and the trees outside the car began to spin. "I need to eat something," he said flatly.

"No problem!" Polunu said cheerfully. "We'll get dinner at Maui's."

"Much as I'd love to gnaw on charred goat heads or roasted palm tree bark or whatever the hell ancient gods eat, I need something *now*. Or we might seriously drive right off this mountain."

"Hey—two more mile markers, and you got the best banana bread on the island."

"Banana bread?"

"Made with the best apple bananas! The *best*! Mmmmm." His big smile plastered his face as he rolled down the window to wave happily to a family standing at a scenic overlook on the side of the road. "*Aloha*, white people!" he called.

"You sure are in a good mood," Gray soured.

"Aren't you?"

He snorted. "Seeing as how a cranky deity from a religion I don't believe in just threw *lava* on me and pretty much sent us to our deaths, no, I'm not really feeling that great."

"No, cuz; you're seeing it wrong! We just survived a meeting with *Pele*! That's cause for celebration! She could have cooked us in her cauldron."

"What a consolation," Gray moaned.

"And she cooled down your shoulder afterward," Polunu pointed out. "And it only hurt for, like, a second right? Looks healed and everything."

"Not the point," Gray snapped, fingering the little hole that Pele had singed into his shirt.

Polunu shrugged. "You'll feel better soon. Banana bread fixes everything, you know?"

"I don't even know what an apple banana is."

"*Tsk-tsk-tsk*," said Polunu. "You need to get out of Missouri."

"I *am* out of Missouri."

"And ain't you having a good time?" he grinned.

"No," Gray confirmed. "So far, the fun has eluded me."

But they did stop for the banana bread, at Polunu's insistence, and Gray had to admit that it did make him happier. A little, at least.

Not long afterward, they saw the sign for a coastal town called Haiku. "Turn off here," Polunu said, nodding toward the ocean. "This is where we find Maui, and our hook." Then, more to himself, he added, "I hope he's in a better mood than Pele was."

Gray eased the car off the highway and rolled along on the small road toward the town. "Okay," he pronounced, "so let's just understand from now on that anytime we talk about gods as if they're real people, it doesn't mean I believe in them, and no matter what happens next, I'm pretty convinced this is all a really complex fever dream."

"It's your trip, cuz," Polunu shrugged. "Call it what you want."

"Having said that, do you honestly think Maui is going to let us borrow his hook to rescue Hi'iaka just because Pele says we need it?"

Polunu shrugged. "Sure, why not? If he's not, like, using it."

Haiku was a sleepy little hippie town full of art galleries and tattoo parlors. Suntanned beach bums hauled boogie boards across the sidewalks and propped them up against the walls before heading in to the thrift stores and taco shacks. Polunu navigated them down the main street, and soon they pulled up in front of a run-down clapboard building overlooking the ocean from its perch on the edge of the coast.

Gray looked up at the faded, weathered sign. "You have *got* to be kidding me," he said.

"What you expect, brah?" Polunu laughed, stepping out of the car. "A beauty parlor?"

"I don't know *what* I expected," Gray sighed, turning off the ignition. "I don't think I know anything about anything anymore." He locked the Corolla, and the two men headed into Maui and Son Fish Company.

"The all-powerful hero of Hawai'ian legend runs a restaurant," Gray murmured, shaking his head as they approached the hostess stand.

"Well, it's not *just* a restaurant. It's a whole fish company."

Gray scratched his brow and closed his eyes. "Of course it is. My mistake."

The hostess seated them on a deck that extended over the ocean. A small fleet of fishing dinghies were tied to the dock below, bobbing dizzily in the water, threatening to tip right over and sink. Gray peered over the railing and raised his eyebrows at the splinted and sun-bleached boats. "I thought fishing boats were...bigger these days."

Polunu shrugged. "I never said it was a *good* fishing company."

The waiter stalked up to the table, his straight, black hair disheveled by the wind. His loose white t-shirt was stained with splatters of grease, and his jeans were ripped through at the knees. He wore a crooked nametag that said Nanamaoa.

"We got ahi and mahi mahi today," the young man started in, "blackened and macadamia nut-crusted. Either one comes with taro chips." Boredom stifled his voice like cotton.

"*Aloha*, cousin! You Maui's son?" Polunu asked. He shifted his weight on the small wooden chair, and it groaned in protest.

"Yeah." He blew a string of hair out of his eyes and tapped his foot impatiently. "Ahi or mahi mahi?"

Polunu leaned in close and wiggled his eyebrows conspiratorially. "He's, like, the *real* Maui, right?"

The waiter rolled his eyes. "Ahi or mahi mahi?" he repeated.

"Hold on, cuz, hold on. This is serious. We gotta speak with your *makuakāne*. He around?"

Nanamaoa exhaled dramatically. "Maui!" he yelled. He turned and slunk back inside the restaurant, heading toward the kitchen. "*Maaaauuuuiiiii!*"

Gray shook his head, watching him go. "Reminds me of my students."

"Hey — you wash dishes for your *makuakāne* for a few thousand years, you see how happy *you* are."

Gray nodded. "Good point."

A few minutes later, a grizzled old man emerged from the bowels of the restaurant. He squinted as he stepped onto the deck and sized up the two men at the table. The old god had long, scraggly hair, gone mostly pepper gray. His skin was deeply tanned and tough as jerky; sea salt filled the creases, streaking him with white hairline stripes from his forehead to the tips of his toes. His right eye bore a scar that began at the eyebrow and tapered off at his cheekbone, and he favored the eye by closing it fully against the sun. He wore a short-sleeve blue button-down shirt opened to the belly and a pair of bedraggled white shorts. The sandals on his feet looked as if they might have once been green, but were now sun-faded to a soft lime white.

He shuffled across the deck and leaned his gnarled hands on the table. "You boys looking for me?" he asked. His voice was sand on a thin sheet of metal.

"Maui-a-kalana!" Polunu gasped. He struggled with his chair, scraping it backward over the wooden planks in short bursts. He banged the table with his knees getting up, knocking over the water glasses and soaking the napkins. He fell to the floor in a mountainous heap and pressed his forehead to the deck. "It is a great honor, *Kupuna* Maui."

The old man scowled at the prostrate Hawai'ian. He nodded down at him and addressed Gray: "What's wrong with your friend?"

"He thinks you're a demigod," Gray replied, mopping up the spilled water.

"Hmpf. He always like this?"

"Maybe. I don't know him that well."

The old man grunted. Then he kicked Polunu under the arm. "Get up, son," he said. Polunu struggled to his feet and plopped back into his chair, out of breath. "Easy, now," the old man soured as the seat threatened to crack. He crossed his ropy arms, covered with white hairs that sprouted through a maze of fading tattoos. "Chairs are expensive."

Polunu was visibly flustered. His shirt stuck to his chest, and he pulled at it nervously. "We need your help, grandfather. We need to—"

"I'm not your grandfather," the old man gruffed.

Polunu screwed up his brow. "But...you *are* Maui...?"

"Yeah, yeah, I'm Maui…no big secret. So?"

"Just to clarify," Gray cut in, "and I'm sorry of this is stupid, but are you the ancient, powerful *demigod* Maui, or just a regular human non-god Maui?"

Maui gritted his teeth. "I'm a fisherman Maui," he said. "That's all." He pulled a pad of paper from his back pocket and clicked a pen out of his lapel. "What are you boys having? We got mahi mahi today, and ahi tuna. Either of them blackened, or else crusted with macadamia…" His voice trailed off as his eyes wandered over the shoulder of Gray's ruined shirt. He shuffled closer and peered down at the burned holes in the cotton. "What do we have here?" he muttered.

Gray frowned down at his wound. "That's sort of why we're here," he said. He gently scooted his chair over toward the railing, putting a bit of distance between himself and the old man. "Um…I was sort of attacked by—"

"Lava burn," Maui said, his gravelly voice hissing between his teeth. He grinned at Gray, a dangerous, sharp-toothed smile. He leaned in closer, and Gray could smell the stench of fish rising from him like a wave. "Now where did you get that?"

"*Tūtū* Pele," Polunu said, leaning forward in his chair. "She sent us to you for help."

The old man grunted again, and some long-hidden memory passed across his eyes. He pulled over a chair from the next table and lowered himself into it gently. "Pele still guards her cauldron, then," he said, a smile playing at the corners of his lips. "Good for her."

"So you *are* the demigod," Gray said.

Polunu scraped his chair backward again, preparing to throw himself back on the ground.

The old man clapped his hand over Polunu's wrist and held it tight, pinning it to the table. "I'm a fisherman," he said through gritted teeth. "Nothing more."

"But we were sent—" Polunu began.

Maui held up his hand. "I'm sure you were. Gods are always sending mortals here, sending mortals there. *Go do this, go do that! Go find Maui...have him slow down the sun! Go get Maui...have him fight the great sea monster! Go get Maui...have him rip apart the earth!* But I'm not that Maui," he said, turning his back on the cleanly healed burns on Gray's shoulder. "All I do is fish."

"Pele's sister's been kidnapped," Polunu blurted.

Maui bared his teeth, and for an instant, Gray could see the fierce and noble young deity that Maui must have been, back when the islands were new. But the moment passed, wiped away by the old man's scowl. "Which sister? Nāmaka? There's one who can take care of herself," he snorted. "The fools who did the kidnapping are the ones who deserve the pity."

"No...not Nāmaka," Polunu replied. "Hi'iaka."

A cloud settled over Maui's brow. "Figures. Pele doesn't have the luck." He spat toward the ocean. It didn't quite make the railing, and it splashed down on the far end of the table instead. Gray blenched. "So. It's the Little Egg who's been taken." He scratched at the tabletop with one thick, warped fingernail. "Too bad. She's a pretty sweet kid."

"Pele has asked us to get her back," Polunu said proudly.

Maui exploded with laughter. The entire deck seemed to shake with the force of it. "*You two* are going to get her back? Well, best of luck, skin bags. What do you want for your last meal?"

"This is *not* making me feel better about things," Gray whispered across the table at Polunu.

"Grandfather Maui—" the large man began.

"Will you *please* stop calling me grandfather?"

"I mean only the deepest respect," Polunu said, bowing his head.

"Oh, you've made that perfectly clear," Maui grumbled. He crossed his arms and stared straight ahead, out toward the gently rolling waves of the horizon. "I don't want your respect. I want to be left alone."

"*Tūtū* Pele sent us to you. She said you would help us."

"Well *Tūtū* Pele was wrong," he said coarsely. "I bet she loved that, didn't she? '*Tūtū*' Pele. I bet she just ate that up."

Gray ran his hands through his hair. He liked having hair, and a scalp to attach it to, but those things would be molten skin and ash if they didn't rescue Hi'iaka. Being stood up at the altar seemed like such a small and insignificant problem now.

His broken honeymoon vacation sure had taken a turn.

"Listen, Maui—" Gray started. Polunu kicked him under the table. "Ow! Sorry! *Mister* Maui. *Grandfather* Maui. *Holiest of all holy* Mauis. Hi'iaka has been taken by some pig-headed god-thing named Kombucha—"

"Kamapua'a," Polunu corrected him.

"—and we only have until tomorrow night to find her. And it's...it's sort of my fault she was taken. If I hadn't—" But he lost his words as he remembered the way she leaned against the railing on the hotel deck, laughing in the dizzying ocean air. "She should have kept running," he finished, "and she didn't, and now we have to get her back." He paused as the weight of it sank into the surface of him, then said it again more firmly: "We *have* to."

Maui smirked. "You sweet on her, mainlander?"

"What?!"

"Hi'iaka. Kid's a looker. Always has been. She snare you in her little web?"

"I don't—that is *not*—" Gray sputtered.

"Yeah," the old god grinned. "She sure got you, all right."

"None of that has anything to do with anything!" Gray exploded. He threw his hands in the air, but that didn't quite seem emphatic enough, so he threw them up again, higher. "And if we don't get her back, Pele's gonna go all Mount Vesuvius on us, *and I am not into that.*"

Maui sat back in his chair and folded his arms across his chest. "Not my concern," he said.

"But you are *akua*," Polunu said, his face falling. "You are *Maui.*"

"I am Maui," the old man said sourly. "So what?"

Polunu looked as if he might cry. "So you're one of the *good* ones. You *help* people." He wrung his great ham-hock hands. "Don't you?"

"No, son; I fish," Maui said. "I run a restaurant. I take people's orders. I keep my head down, and I mind my own business. You boys should have done the same."

"How can you say that?" Polunu said. "You are *Maui*!"

"You keep saying that, but it doesn't mean what you think it does." He spat again, and this time the glob made it over the railing. Gray sighed with relief. "You know what happens when you meddle in the petty bickering of *nā akua*?"

"You get lava burn," Gray grumped, "and a hole in your favorite t-shirt."

Maui nodded and stubbed his finger on the tabletop. "At *best.* The gods get their hackles up, and bloody chaos reigns until they've battered each other into the ground. People get killed, homes get destroyed, whole villages drown, and the earth falls apart. For what? For family squabbles. Wounded pride. Battles over territory that was never theirs to begin with. Kamapua'a gets captured by an evil chicken, and eight hundred men get slaughtered when he's set free. Pele sleeps with Nāmaka's husband, and Hawai'i's volcanoes get doused to cold dust. Kanaloa teaches a few kids magic, and all hell breaks loose. The world isn't a better place because of *nā akua*," he said. "It's a better place because we've all been forgotten."

Gray shifted in his seat and gazed out over the ocean. The old man's words rang with truth; every mythology was filled to overflowing with insignificant arguments among the gods that resulted in havoc and death for the people who worshipped them. History knew no limit of the stories that ended in tragedy for the mortals who got trampled under the feet of the immortals.

But those weren't the only stories.

"The gods have done plenty of good things, though," he said. Then, remembering his severely limited experience with Polynesian mythos, he added, "I assume."

"Yes," Polunu nodded. "The gods *have* done good things. *You* have done good things!"

"Ancient history," the old man growled.

"You are Maui, who fished the islands of Hawai'i up from the ocean floor!"

"A mistake."

"You are Maui, who pushed up the skies to make room for humans to live!"

"A bigger mistake."

"You are *MAUI*," Polunu said, shouting now, as he pushed his seat back and stood up, towering above the old god, "who roped the sun while it slept and harnessed it so you could drag it back and slow its movement across the sky so we could have longer days to grow our food and live in light! You have done more to help Hawai'ians than almost anybody! And there's a Hawai'ian who needs your help right now!" And then, just to be clear, he added, "That Hawai'ian is me."

"And what was my reward for doing all that?" the grizzled old god said, his face darkening. "A pat on the head and a list of patronizing titles: Maui the Trickster; Maui the Half-God; Maui the World's Worst Fisherman. But even the jeering was better than their apathy, boy. Yes, I raised the sky on my shoulders. Yes, I fished up the islands. Yes, I dragged down the sun. I killed the eight-eyed bat, and I brought the humans their fire, and a thousand other feats besides. Yet the people of Hawai'i moved on without *nā akua*…they left us here to wither in the sun."

"But you just said they were better off without you," Gray said.

"They *are* better off!" Maui exploded, slamming a fist down on the table. "And good for them! They turned their backs so readily, and everything's working out for them like sunshine and blossoms. I don't need their love. I don't need their thanks. I turn my back on *them*, too, and all of us are better for it. You understand? The people do what the people will. I fish, and I run my restaurant, and I do not get involved."

An uneasy silence fell over the table. Gray found himself looking at his hands, shamed by the old god's words, though he personally hadn't forgotten Maui. He never even knew about him in the first place.

He felt that might be even worse.

But regardless of Maui's feelings, Gray and Polunu had a job to do.

"You don't have to get involved," Gray said quietly, still lost in the important intricacies of his own fingers. "We just need to borrow your hook."

Maui looked at him. Then he looked at Polunu. Then he looked back at Gray.

"I imagine you're joking, son. But your punch line needs work."

"I'm not joking," Gray said, shaking his head. He still didn't chance a look in Maui's direction. "If we can borrow the hook, we can go and leave you to your fish."

"You want to borrow Manaiakalani," Maui said, bewildered. "You want to just...*borrow* it."

Polunu shrugged. "We'll bring it right back." Maui gave him a look. "I mean, if we don't die."

Maui snorted. "*There's* the trick of it," he said.

"*Tūtū* Pele sent us to you to ask for your blessing. She said you might lend us Manaiakalani to defeat Kamapua'a."

"Neither my blessing nor my hook is hers to give," Maui shot back.

"That's why we came, grandfa—um, Maui. *Tūtū* Pele said you are our best chance. That you are our *only* chance. I beg you to open your heart to us and grant us your favor." He lowered his eyes. "I'd really like to see my pineapple stand again."

"You want to wield my ancestral hook as a weapon against the demigod pig-man? Do you boys even know what Manaiakalani would do to a creature like Kamapua'a?" Maui asked.

Gray raised an eyebrow at Polunu.

Polunu shrugged. "Well...not really," he admitted.

"Of course not," Maui scoffed. "Pele wants you to hook Kamapua'a right in the chest, and then Pele wants you to yank the hook back out, because Pele knows that when you do, you'll draw out the divine soul of him, leaving him mortal and vulnerable. Which is exactly what *Pele* wants, because *Pele* would like to never deal with that wretch ever again, and *Pele* works her little web, doesn't she? Oh, yes, she does. She just can't keep her fingers out of every basket, no matter who has to pay the price." Maui clenched his jaw against some old memory that threatened to bubble to the surface. "What Pele wants, Pele seems to get."

An uncomfortable silence fell over the table. Finally, Gray cleared his throat. "I see what you're saying here," he said slowly, "and you seem to not really be into the whole 'do Pele's bidding' thing. But...I mean, the whole part about draining his divinity sounds like it would work pretty well...right?"

Maui grunted. "Sure. It'd work just fine, if you could manage it."

"Okay. So Pele may be selfish, but she's also not wrong. If this is the only way we can face King Pig, we at least have to try." Then he added softly, "We can't just abandon Hi'iaka."

Maui shook his head and sighed. "Draining his immortality sounds great and all. But son, do you think Kamapua'a *wants* to become mortal?"

Gray considered that. "No," he decided, "I don't suppose he does." Being immortal and omnipotent sounded like a pretty good gig.

"So do you think he's very likely to allow that to happen?"

"Look, I don't expect him to be thrilled about it," Gray said, suddenly feeling very tired. He rubbed at the corners of his eyes.

"But we don't have a whole lot of choices here. Either we do it and we save her, or we die trying, or we die from *not* trying. Those are our options. I don't like any of them, and I should have stayed at the hotel this morning and sent Pele her message in the mail and let all you *akua* work out your own stupid problems, but I didn't, because I'm an idiot, and because she smelled like coconut, and the sand crabs really weirded me out, and now here we are, and can we please borrow your fish hook to save Hi'iaka from a deranged half-pig god thing?!"

Polunu gasped, horrified at the way Gray had spoken to the revered god of Polynesia and father of Hawai'i. But Maui, for his part, only gritted his teeth and dug his fingers into the table wood, lost in thought. Finally he said, "If you can retrieve it, you can use it to save the Little Egg, or die trying. But mark my words, mainlander: if it's not returned to me in pristine condition, Pele's lake of fire will look like the pleasant option."

Polunu smiled with relief. He pressed his hands together and bobbed his head in gratitude. "*Mahalo,* Maui. *Mahalo nui loa!*"

"Wait, wait, *wait*—back up a second," Gray said, holding up his hand. "If we can *retrieve* it?"

Maui flashed a grin. "We'll see how bad you want to save your Hi'iaka, *haole.*"

"What does that mean?" Gray's heart sank. "Where exactly is this magical hook?"

Maui's grin stretched even wider. "I hope you're not afraid of sharks."

# Chapter 10

"I hate everyone, and I hate everything, and I am never coming back to Hawai'i," Gray muttered.

"Relax, brah," Polunu said. "It's just a day at the beach. You white people come to Hawai'i for the ocean, right?" He gestured out over the water. "Here it is."

They stood at the end of the old pier, its heavy wooden planks stained dark by water and slimy with algae. Maui stood on the deck of his restaurant a few hundred feet up the beach, nodding at them encouragingly...or maybe he was being patronizing. It was hard to tell at that distance.

Gray peered over the edge of the dock. There it was: the legendary Manaiakalani, the great Hook of Maui that had dredged up the islands of Hawai'i from the ocean floor all those millennia ago. It was so unassuming, lying there in the sand beneath the lazy waters, and not nearly as big as Gray expected—only about two feet long from handle to curve. Covered in sand and barnacles, it was little more than a shadowy outline of bone at the bottom of the ocean, but it was unmistakable. All that stood between Gray and Maui's hook was about four feet of water.

Four feet of water, and a tangle of primeval half-shark sea monsters.

"What *are* those things?" Gray asked, disgusted. There must have been two dozen of them writhing around in the water. They looked like sharks, with gray skin, lolling eyes, razor-sharp teeth, and short, triangular fins...but they also had rough scales, and arms wriggling out from behind their heads, and each arm had three webbed fingers with long, black nails. Their tailfins were fixed with curved six-inch barbs. They struggled over each other, clawing their way around in knots, swinging their tails and snapping their jaws any time they got tangled among one another.

"Protectors. Guardians of Manaiakalani. Not the shark god's little demons, I don't think," Polunu said, frowning down at the water. "Something different. Something new." He straightened up to his full height and gave Gray a shrug. "I don't know," he said.

"I thought you were supposed to know everything. I thought you could feel it in your heart," Gray snapped, stabbing a finger into Polunu's chest. "What happened to your heart, Polunu?!"

"My heart is full of love for *nā akua*," he replied, scratching his arm. "But I don't know *what* these things are."

"Thanks. Great. Very helpful."

"Just go in quick," he said encouragingly, putting his arm around Gray's shoulder as the smaller man struggled to stand under the weight of it. "Like stealing a pineapple."

Gray blinked up at the big Hawai'ian. "How is this *at all* like stealing a pineapple?" he demanded.

"You ain't never stolen a pineapple before?"

"No!"

"Well that's good. 'Cause stealing is wrong. But we have a saying in my neighborhood: 'You gonna steal a pineapple, you better move like a lizard.'"

Gray shook his head and sighed. "I can't even begin to guess what that means."

"It means pineapples are very important to the farmer, and he watches them close, you know? So you want to steal one, you better move like a lizard—blend in, be quick, stay low to the ground. Otherwise, the farmer, he catch you and stab you with a stick."

Gray just stood and stared.

"It's a very sharp stick," Polunu explained.

"I bet."

"So you gonna get Manaiakalani, you gotta be quick, like a lizard. Otherwise, you get the farmer's stick." He tilted his head back out over the water and curled his lips at the creatures below. "In this case, it's the shark's mouth, I guess."

"I got it. Thanks."

"Yeah, I'd avoid the tail, too," Polunu continued. He pointed down into the water. "Some of those spikes look like they got black on them, see? That might be poison. Probably not so good for you."

"How can sharks have *arms*?" Gray said. He was glad he hadn't eaten any fish up at Maui's; it would all be coming back up right about now.

"They ain't sharks, braddah. Might've started out that way, but they ain't that way anymore. They got dark magic inside."

"Why can't anything be easy?" Gray sighed, pinching the bridge of his nose.

"What'd you think it'd be like?" Polunu asked, shooting him that wide, lopsided grin. "I thought you said you teach mythology."

Gray took a few deep breaths to try to clear his mind. He inhaled the strong, salty scent of the ocean, and he let his gaze wander down the coast of Maui to the sharp, verdant mountains rising through the haze in the distance. "You know, Hawai'i would be a really nice place if it wasn't trying to kill me so hard," he mused.

"Everything worth loving is worth working hard for," Polunu pointed out.

Gray nodded. "Okay. I'm going for it." He jerked a thumb over his shoulder. "Hand me that oar."

Polunu screwed up his face in confusion, but he trotted off down the pier, picked up an oar that had been left on the planks, and handed it over. "What you gonna do with that?"

"I'm gonna hook the hook," Gray said, shaking out his arms and popping his neck. "Stand back. I'm going for it."

Polunu took two steps back. Gray paused, then waved the Hawai'ian closer. "Never mind, come back. If I start to fall, you grab me."

"What do you mean, if you start to fall? Ain't you going in?"

"In *there*?" Gray cried, jabbing the oar toward the evil sharks. "Hell no! I'm just gonna...you know..." He wiggled the oar through the air. "Flip it up."

Polunu squinted and scratched his head. "I don't think that's gonna work, *haole*. Maui said you need to get in the water."

"Well with an oar, I don't *have* to get in the water," Gray said irritably.

"Yeah, but this is probably, like, a test or something, don't you think?"

"Look, why are you fighting me on this? Are you going to help me or not?"

"I guess so. What you want me to do?"

"Hold my shirt. Don't let me fall in."

"You got it, brah." He grabbed the back of Gray's t-shirt with such force, Gray pitched forward with a screech and nearly toppled over the edge of the pier. But Polunu held firm.

Gray stuck out over the water, wheeling his arms in panic. The oar swung around and nearly bashed Polunu in the head. "Pull me back, pull me back!" he screamed.

Polunu reeled him back in. "Sorry." The big man blushed, wiggling his fingers in the air. "Clumsy hands, you know?"

Gray glowered up at him. "Hey. I have a new idea. Why don't *you* get the stupid hook?"

"Nah. We have another saying, when it comes to dangerous things like this: 'Let the mainlander do it.'"

"Okay. Okay." Gray closed his eyes and inhaled, exhaled...inhaled...exhaled. "Let's get this over with." He dropped to his knees and crawled to the edge of the pier. Then he lay down on his belly and stretched the oar out over the water. "If they pull me in, find a gun and shoot me."

He lowered the oar into the water and pushed it down toward the hook. He winced as he threaded the paddle through the squirming throng of shark-monsters. They bumped and slithered up against the wood, and he paused with a sharp breath...but they continued to swim around it, and he resumed easing it down toward the hook. He pushed until his arm was fully extended, but the edge of the paddle was still a few inches away from the curve of the hook. He wriggled himself out a little further over the edge of the pier, until his chest was hovering above the water. He gripped the wood beneath his belly with his free hand and pushed the oar further in. "Come on," he whispered, the tip of the paddle quivering just centimeters away from the hook. "Come on..."

He pulled his hand back on the oar so he was gripping just the knob on the end. He pushed the oar down, and it scraped against the inside curve of the hook.

The shark-monsters flew into a frenzy. They screamed beneath the water, and their shrieks broke the surface as a choked, garbled cacophony, like nails against stone. They swarmed the handle of the oar, wrapping their sickly fingers around it and pulling it down into the water. Gray was caught off-guard and went tumbling forward off the pier with a cry of surprise. Polunu caught him by the waistband of his shorts before he plunged into the ocean. He hung there, suspended, while the demons dug their teeth into the oar and snapped it in half.

"Pull me up, pull me up!" Gray cried.

He kept hold of his end of the handle as Polunu dragged him back onto the dock, with three of the shark monsters holding on. Their eyes flashed up at the human pair through the water, and they began pulling their way up the handle, hand over hand. One broke through the water and screamed; Gray could see down its red throat through three rows of pointy, glass-sharp teeth. The thing writhed and twisted like a creature in pain. It scrabbled up the oar and swiped its claws at Gray's wrist. Gray screamed and dropped the handle, and the creature missed by less than an inch. Polunu yanked him back onto the pier, and they tumbled backward. Gray bounced off of Polunu's belly and rolled across the pier, almost falling clear off the other side. He slapped his hands onto the wet wood and pulled himself back into the center, breathing hard.

"Well," Polunu said, gazing up at the blue sky, "that did not work."

"No. It...did not," Gray agreed.

They struggled to their feet. Gray looked back up at the fish house. Maui waved down, and though he couldn't be sure, Gray felt pretty confident the old man was smiling.

"What you wanna do now, cuz?"

Gray gritted his teeth. "I want to get that hook," he said, glaring up at the old god on the deck. "Because nothing is impossible, dammit." He straightened his shirt and marched back to the end of the pier. The shark-monsters had stopped frothing through the water, and the surface was calm.

"You're gonna go in?" Polunu asked, surprised.

"We're out of options, and you're a baby and won't do it for me," Gray said. He raised his arms straight up in the air. "Come over here and lower me down."

"If you say so, brah." He lumbered over and clasped Gray's wrists. "You sure about this?"

"Nope."

"What if you get eaten?"

"What if you don't make me think about it?"

Polunu frowned. "Hey, if this goes bad...I mean...it's good to know you, you know?" He sniffled back a tear. "You're not so smart, you know, but you got a good heart."

Gray snorted. "Thanks. That's...well. Thanks. And you're really big, and I was basically terrified of you when you force-fed me pineapple, but you're a good person, Polunu. That's pretty rare." He slapped the man gently on the cheek. "I'll see you in a minute."

Polunu smiled. "See you in a minute, brah."

Then he lifted Gray like he was a rag doll and dipped him into the ocean.

"Slower!" Gray cried, his indifferent bravado melting away like chipped ice in the summer sun. "Take my sandals!" He kicked his feet and flung the flip-flops up onto the dock. It occurred to him that he hadn't really thought this through. "My shirt's gonna get wet," he said, closing his eyes as his feet plunged into the lukewarm sea.

But a wet shirt was pretty much the least of his problems.

He held his breath as Polunu lowered him down, and he felt a rough patch of skin slither against his ankles. He shuddered and suddenly couldn't fill his lungs with enough air to feed his blood. A second shark monster brushed against his shin, and then a third. He felt the gentle scrape of nails against his flesh, and the smooth glide of a poisoned barb against his calf.

"Should I stop?" Polunu whispered, afraid of upsetting the creatures.

"No," Gray wheezed, struggling to catch his breath. "Like a lizard. Just go fast."

"Okay," said Polunu, sounding uncertain. Then he let go of Gray's wrists, and the *haole* fell into the ocean.

He plunged through the mass of writhing Shark-things. His knees buckled when he hit sand, and for a few moments, he was completely submerged. The creatures twisted around his waist and his shoulders, skimmed his neck with their claws, brushed their barbs through his hair. He pushed himself off the bottom of the ocean and burst up through the surface, gasping for air. The sea monsters thrashed around him, hissing and snapping their powerful jaws. Gray stood as still as a trembling oak. The guardians of Manaiakalani began to swim around him in a tight, slow circle.

"What are they doing?" Gray hissed, keeping his voice low.

"They got you surrounded!" Polunu wailed.

"How far am I from the hook?"

"It's right behind you, brah. *Right* behind you."

"Okay." Gray's breath began to come more easily. The sharks were circling, but they weren't attacking. "Okay. Okay. Don't make a sound."

He bent his right knee and slowly pulled up his foot. His heel brushed against a monster, and the creature snapped at his foot. A tooth sliced through his skin just below his toes, and he cursed between his teeth. He moved his foot more carefully, more slowly, back toward the hook. He felt the hard, uneven surface of it beneath his toes. The shark-things became more frantic, thrashing their tails as they circled, and drawing themselves in, tightening the ring. Gray passed his toes over the curve of the hook and dug them into the sand on the far side. The sea monsters began to scream beneath the water, and they reared back and snapped at his arms and chest. He seized up in fear, but they seemed to be testing him; they didn't bite him, and they didn't scratch, but they rammed their heads up against him, as if trying him for weakness. Tears began to spill out of the corners of his eyes, but he pressed on, tunneling his toes beneath the hook. He lifted his foot, and Manaiakalani came with it, peeling up from the sand. One of the creatures thrashed its way to the surface and lifted its horrible head. It curved its spine and raised itself to Gray's height and opened its mouth...he was just inches away from the triangular teeth that dripped with water and foam. Gray squeezed his eyes shut and tilted his head back, away from the monster. He lifted the hook up through the water, and the creatures began to nip at his foot. He cracked open one eye, and the slavering shark-monster before him began gnashing its jaws, flinging strings of spit and saltwater against Gray's cheek. The monster snapped its teeth, then hinged its jaw open wide and dove forward, lunging at Gray's face. Gray plunged his hand down and grabbed Manaiakalani, grasping it around the curve. He hauled it out of the water and held it up like a shield.

As soon as his hand seized the hook, the monsters stopped thrashing. They suddenly became docile and quiet, and they began to sink through the water. They floated down to the sand, and even the shark that had been gnashing just inches from Gray's eyes went slack and fell against him weakly, like its batteries had just died. It fell back into the ocean with a quiet splash and drifted away with the pull of the waves.

Gray opened one eye. Then he opened the other. "What did I just do?" he whispered, staring down in amazement at the blanket of sleeping sea monsters at the bottom of the ocean.

"You silenced the water demons," Polunu said, equally confused. "I think maybe you passed the test! And braddah, you are holding the Hook of Maui."

Gray lifted the hook out of the water. Crusted with age but still smooth to the touch, jagged and sharp but elegantly curved, Manaiakalani gleamed in the sunshine when Gray scraped the scales away and thrummed with a primeval power that he could feel tingling through his entire body. "This is the weirdest day of my life," he breathed.

"Sure is," Polunu said, wiping a tear of joy from his eye. "Think we earned some mahi mahi, yeah?"

"Oh my God, I'm so hungry," Gray laughed. He waded back toward the pier, and Polunu helped him out of the water.

"We'll eat up, cousin," Polunu said, giving Gray a big, squishy hug. "Big dinner for both of us. *Big* dinner! Gotta build up that strength!" He patted his belly happily. "Gotta be prepared, you know? We got an uphill climb from here."

"That's great," Grey said sarcastically, heading back toward land. "I was definitely hoping it would only get worse."

# Chapter 11

Hi'iaka spat into the dirt. "You are a coward," she declared, thrusting out her chin.

"I am your god and your king; your *akua* and *ali'i*. I will not be spoken to with such a tongue." Her captor stepped forward from the shadows, and light from the ceiling fell across his shoulders, revealing his true face: gray-brown fur, a blunt snout flanked by two upturned tusks, and two beady, wide-set eyes sunken below a pair of triangular ears. Kamapua'a carried himself like a man, and had the lean, muscular body of a true god, but he had the head a wild boar perched atop his powerful shoulders. Hi'iaka did not draw back from his grotesque face, but stood at the very front edge of her circle, her hands planted on her hips.

"Remember that you are a guest in my home," he warned, drool spilling out from beneath his tusks. "I need you alive, but only just."

"Why?" Hi'iaka shot back. "Will you bargain with me to win back the love of your former wife?"

"*Pele has nothing to do with this!*" he squealed, and the sounder of boars near the fire took up the call, screeching and screaming into the flames. "She is a petty, small-minded *pelapela* dog!" He stamped his feet like a child in a tantrum.

Hi'iaka smiled. "She is more powerful than you can ever hope to be, and soon she will come to set me free. And this time, she will roast you alive."

Kamapua'a snorted. He reached up to the top of his head and pulled his hands down his face, wiping away his true form and leaving his human face in its wake. He was undeniably handsome as a human, with wavy black hair, high, strong cheekbones, large brown eyes, and a small, pinched mouth. But when he smiled, he revealed lower canines that were small, sharp boar tusks, and there was never any mistaking the animal rage in his eyes. "You and I both know that she will not leave her little fire pit—not even to rescue her precious little sister. Pele cares more for her rocks than she does for you, sweetling."

"She will send a great warrior," Hi'iaka said smugly, crossing her arms and standing firm. "She will infuse him with her power, and he will set me free, and you will be destroyed."

"Darling dreams, child. But in case she does, I've taken certain measures to stop any hero that might be foolish enough to try. And as for Pele's power..." He gave her that razor smile now. "Soon that will change. That is why you're here."

"Your *mana* does not have the power to withstand Pele," Hi'iaka sneered.

Kamapua'a squealed with laughter. "That comes right to the point, does it not? My power is great, but bends like cane to the tiresome Pele. But if I double my *mana*, then I will have the power to douse the fire of Pele, and of any other who would challenge me. All of Polynesia will fall to its knees before the hog-god Kamapua'a. I will rule our islands and spread terror to the countries who have raped and ravaged our land."

"Double your *mana*?" Hi'iaka laughed. "You are the fool you have always been, Lord of Pigs. The life force of every single human on Earth would not give you the strength to destroy my sister."

"Humans," Kamapua'a snorted. "Mortals. As worthless as they are pathetic."

"Then where will you find this magical *mana*?"

Kamapua'a grinned. His eyes bore black holes into Hi'iaka. "Somewhere quite close to home, I think."

Hi'iaka scoffed. "You cannot be serious."

"As serious as death."

"I am no weak-willed human. I am not even a floundering *demi*god, like you, pig-lord. I am the daughter of Haumea and Kāne. I am the goddess of sorcery and medicine, of hula and chant; the patron goddess of Hawai'i itself. The thunder and lightning are in my charge. You think you will take my *mana*, demigod? You are a pathetic, laughable wretch. I am no ignorant *hûpô*. My shadow will not give up its power. I am Hi'iaka-i-ka-poli-o-Pele," she hissed, "and I will not succumb."

Kamapua'a, startled, drew back a step, recoiling from her venom. Then his face regained composure, and he gave his prisoner a satisfied smirk. "And yet, for all your power, you are wholly contained by a circle scratched into the dirt. You think you will not succumb? Well, we will see, Little Egg," he said, laughing and turning his back. "We will see."

He faded back into his true face and joined his of army of pigs around the fire.

# Chapter 12

Gray sat bolt upright in bed. The sheets were damp with sweat, and his heart pounded against his chest. He looked wildly around the room; it was dark, and quiet, and unbelievably comfortable. He was in his bed at the Hyatt.

"Oh my God," he wheezed. He placed a hand over his heart and willed it to slow before it burst straight through his skin. Then he laughed. "I'm in my room," he said, falling back against his pillow and spreading his arms across the bed. "It was all a dream!"

"I got dreams too, braddah. Weird stuff."

Gray screamed and leapt out of his bed. Polunu sat up slowly from his spot on the floor, rubbing his eyes and yawning. "You okay, cuz?"

Reality slowly settled back on Gray's shoulders, weighing them down as he sank into a seat on the bed. "Yeah," he said miserably, burying his face in his hands. "Everything is fine and dandy. And real. Everything is real, too."

"No mistaking that!" the Hawai'ian said cheerfully. "I was right. Sleeping in a hotel is *much* better than sleeping in a van!"

The memory of the previous night rushed into Gray's mind like a freight train. After finally sitting down to dinner at Maui and Son, the sky was beginning to grow dark, with the sun sinking quickly toward the horizon. "Think we can still make it tonight?" Gray asked. After his encounters with Pele, Maui, and the shark-monsters, he was eager to either get the girl or get dead trying.

"No way," Polunu said, wiping dried flakes of smashed sweet potatoes from the corners of his lips. "We can't get to the upcountry before dark. We gotta take a different road around the mountain. It'll take a while. And believe me...you don't wanna be in the upcountry after dark." The big man shuddered.

Gray felt a chill of his own tingle down his spine. "What's the plan, then?" he asked, throwing a few bills down on the table and heading toward the car. "You need a ride back to your van?"

"You wanna crash in my van?" Polunu asked, raising an eyebrow.

"Ha!" Gray snorted. "No. I want *you* to crash in your van, and I want *me* to sleep in my hotel room, which was way too expensive to not be slept in."

"Hmm," Polunu said, rubbing his chin. "You're at the Hyatt, yeah? On Kā'anapali?"

"Yeah."

Polunu nodded. "Then I'll just go with you."

"Oooh, no," Gray said, holding up his hands. "You can go back to your van, and I'll pick you up in the morning."

"But that don't make sense!" Polunu protested. "You'd have to come all the way to this side of the island just to go all the way back. Nah...it's better if I stay with you."

"No way. Absolutely not."

"It'll be fun!" the big Hawai'ian grinned. "Like a sleepover!"

"Huh-uh. No, sir." Gray shook his head. "There is only one bed, and I am sleeping in it. *Alone.*"

"That's okay," Polunu shrugged. "I'll take the floor."

"You're gonna hate that," Gray said, feeling himself giving in.

"No way! I'm gonna *love* it," Polunu beamed.

Now, sitting on the bed and frowning down at his new room-mate, Gray grimaced as he worked to pop his back. "Well? Did you love it?"

"It was the *best*," Polunu confirmed. And he sounded like he meant it.

They grabbed oatmeal and coffee from the cafe in the lobby be-fore heading out to the car. "You got a nice place here, cuz," Polunu said, gazing up in wonder at the towering hotel.

"Don't get used to it," Gray grumbled, fishing for his keys. "We'll probably both be dead before we ever make it back."

With Polunu navigating, they sped toward the rising sun and the upcountry in the east. The landscape changed dramatically as they left Lahaina behind, fading from verdant hill slopes to a harsh, brutal land of red soil spotted with low brush that looked like gi-ant mold spores against the mountainside. Then the world became lush again as they drove up Highway 380, and Gray shook his head as they approached the sprawling sugarcane fields of the expansive Maui flatland.

"It's like every single type of landscape in the world came to retire on Maui," he said.

"Every type of landscape in the world comes to *live* on Maui," Polunu corrected him, giving the sugarcane a quiet salute. "The is-land provides all the things we need, and the things we don't know we need, too."

"Which part of you needs a Big Mac?" Gray asked, nodding toward a McDonald's off the highway.

"Well," Polunu said sadly, acknowledging the double arches, "the island can't control everything."

Polunu directed them onto a new highway, and they doubled back south toward the lower part of the eastern half of the island. "So where exactly are we going?" Gray asked. "Where is this fabled 'upcountry'?"

"The upcountry is *up*," Polunu replied, looking at Gray as if he'd just asked what color clouds were. "For an English teacher, you don't know what words mean too much."

"And for an English-speaker, you don't know how sentences work too much," Gray shot back.

They wound their way along the rising mountainside, with the Pacific Ocean glimmering in the morning sun to their right. The water was a startling blue and looked as smooth as a mirror from their altitude. Gray worked hard to forget the fact that there was about a 90% chance that this would be his last day on Earth, but he didn't do a very good job of it. He just drank in the view as he drove, desperately willing himself to remember it. *This is the beauty the world can have*, he told himself. *This is why it's worth at least* trying *to survive.*

The Hook of Maui had been tossed unceremoniously into the back, where it had bounced off the seat and become wedged between the middle console and the floor. "How do you think we use that thing?" Gray asked, motioning toward the hook with a nod of his head. "Just, like, jam it in his chest?"

Polunu shrugged. "We could always stab him through the neck," he suggested.

Gray drew back his head and made a disgusted face. "Geez, Polunu. That's...intense."

"Just leaving all options open, cuz." Gray could tell by his tone that he meant it, and intense or not, he was glad to have the Hawai'ian along for the adventure.

"What's the upcountry like? Aside from being 'up'?"

Polunu frowned. He shifted in his seat, his left arm crushing into Gray's driving hand as the Corolla veered across the highway. "Hey!" Gray cried, jerking the car back onto the right side of the road.

"Sorry," Polunu said, casting his eyes down. "I'm just too big."

"Tell me about it," Gray grumbled.

"The upcountry, though...don't really know what to expect, *haole*. They don't really care for mainlanders up there. They got their own thing goin' on, you know? Got sort of hard feelings against tourists and *nā haole* who come to Hawai'i and build ten-million dollar homes on the beach and complain about how many locals we got. In the upcountry, they sort of got their own rules. Their own gods, too."

"Their own gods?"

"That's right, braddah. The upcountry gods go way back, and they ain't tied to the big gods. More angry, more *primal*, you know?" He shrugged. "That's what the stories say, anyway."

"Sounds like fun," Gray muttered dryly.

"It ain't fun at all," Polunu replied seriously. "Sometimes even when locals go up to the country, then don't come back at all."

Gray shook his head. "Thanks. I was joking, but...thanks."

"Just want you to know what you gettin' into. The upcountry folk don't come down to town much. Live in seclusion, you know? It does things to the brain, I think." He held a finger up to his temple and swirled it around. "Scrambles you a little. Makes you weird sometimes. Maybe makes you dangerous, too."

"Great. So we're headed up into the mountains to face a bunch of lunatics who hate mainlanders and worship angry gods. Anything else I should know?"

Polunu thought a second. "They got lots of guns."

"Oh good. Just perfect. So glad I woke up for this."

"We should have brought lunch," Polunu mused, staring out at the ocean.

"We're driving into a band of gun-toting hill people to find a wild, powerful pig-god who's almost definitely going to rip us to pieces, and you're thinking about lunch?"

"Dinner, too. What if we're still up there and we miss dinner?" he sighed.

"I wouldn't worry too much about it, considering you'll probably *be* dinner for a wild pig-god."

"Nah. Kamapua'a and his pigs, they eat *you*, maybe, but not me." He patted his great belly. "Bacon and me, we got an understanding."

The hills were green and lush as they passed through the center of the island, but the landscape changed again as they wrapped around the southern coast of the harshly sloping mountains, and on the left, stretching toward the peaks, the earth became suddenly barren and rocky and bright, rusty red. The wind kicked up eddies of dirt, forming little red tornadoes that whipped across the mountain. It was quiet, and desolate, and distinctly Martian. Gray was amazed that the land could change so quickly, and so completely.

But that was the left side of the road. The land on the right side was still green, covered with a thick layer of tall grass that swayed in the breeze, all the way down to the rough ocean cliffs.

It was Mars on one side, the Great Plains on the other, with the paved highway bisecting the two halves perfectly.

"It's beautiful, no?" Polunu grinned, watching Gray's face. "My Hawai'i is a special place. Nowhere like her on Earth."

Gray nodded as the landscape unfurled before them. Maui was nothing if not breathtaking in its beauty, and each new terrain was a blunt reminder that the island was in charge.

"How will we know where to find this pig-god? And Hi'ia-ka?" Gray asked. His moonlit meeting with the gorgeous goddess seemed so long ago now, and he was startled when he realized only two nights had passed since. And if their meeting was ages ago, his own engagement and failed wedding was someone else's lifetime. A different sort of tragedy that had happened to a different sort of person.

The world had changed so much since then.

"We gotta follow the pigs," Polunu replied.

"Okay. Sure. Follow the pigs. Makes sense. To find the pig-god, follow the pigs. I am actively deciding to buy into that idea," he proclaimed aloud, just to prove to both Polunu and himself just how open-minded he was being about this brand-new world of gods and pigs. "And how exactly do we find them?"

"We keep our eyes open. And we hope the gods are on our side."

Traffic was practically non-existent at this time of the morning, aside from the occasional pickup truck that blasted past them at 70 miles an hour. There were more goats on the road than cars, and more than once, Gray had to ease the Corolla to a stop while they waited for an errant herd to wander across the highway.

"You see?" Polunu said. "I told you. Goats."

"You also said the road on the other side would be worse. But this is a smooth dream, my friend."

Polunu snorted. "You just wait, cuz. This road is *much* worse than the other one. You just wait."

As if on cue, trees reappeared on the mountain, and the dry desert faded into the rearview. The road ramped up to higher elevations and completely fell apart; the smooth, paved surface gave way to a deeply rutted, pocked disaster. The car bumped and bounced and rattled as they crept along, and the higher they got, the closer the road ran to the edge of the cliff. It was only wide enough for one car, with curves that wrapped around the mountain like ribbon. There had once been a guardrail, but it had long ago rusted away, and only the stark, naked metal posts jutted up through the rock. There was nothing to stop the car from pitching over the sheer edge of the mountain.

"Who is in charge of your Department of Transportation?!" Gray cried, holding onto the wheel for dear life.

"What, you think the mountain's gonna lay down so you can put a nice, flat road on it?" Polunu asked with a laugh. He gave Gray a wink. "Try not to be such a *haole, haole.*"

"I don't wanna die in a rental car," Gray whimpered.

As they crawled up the mountain, the clouds knitted themselves together overhead, and rain began to spatter across the windshield. Gray gripped the wheel even tighter and slowed the car to a glacial pace. "See any pigs yet?" he asked, desperate to get off the road.

"Not pigs," Polunu said, pointing through the windshield. "But I *do* see breakfast."

"We already had breakfast."

"So what? You can't ever have too many breakfasts."

A small gravel lot opened up on the left. Through the drizzling rain, Gray could just make out a faded, hand-painted sign that said Auntie Alina's Country Provisions. Gray exhaled with relief as he pulled off the road and rolled to a stop in front of the little green shack. "Probably too much to hope for a breakfast burrito, huh?" he said, peering up at the rundown building.

"It's never wrong to hope," Polunu said. He peeled himself out of the car and headed inside.

"Right," Gray sighed. "Hope is the best." He tucked Maui's hook out of sight. Then he ducked through the rain and followed Polunu into the roadside stand. There was no electricity in the shack; the only light came in through the open-air windows, but with the sky clouded over, not much sunlight filtered into the room. Rows of shelves had been inexpertly nailed into three of the walls, and a handmade, uneven counter was loosely fixed to the fourth. A slight, older woman stood behind the counter, her long, stringy hair hanging down in front of her thin face. She was almost impossible to distinguish from the shadows.

"*Aloha!*" Polunu called, waving to the woman.

"*Aloha,*" she replied.

"Beautiful weather, yeah?" Polunu said, shaking the water from his big, sleeveless sail of a shirt.

"Rain makes the taro grow," she said curtly.

Polunu nodded. "Yes it does," he agreed.

Gray stalked around the shelves, squinting at the produce through the gloom. The selection was sparse—a small basket of soft-skinned lilikoi, several browning bunches of the tiny bananas, a few plastic bags of homemade taro chips, three loaves of molding banana bread, three crates of wilting mangos, a sad stack of squishy avocados, and about half a dozen papayas. Gray grimaced as he inspected the mangos and was greeted by a swarm of fruit flies buzzing angrily around the crates. In the end, he settled for three of the bananas and a bag of the taro chips. Polunu grabbed up the three least-rotten mangos and a whole papaya.

"How are you planning on eating that?" Gray asked, nodding at the papaya.

Polunu tilted his head in confusion. "With my mouth," he said. "You know?"

Gray rolled his eyes. "Yes, I understand that, but how are you going to cut it open?"

Polunu shrugged. "I'll use a rock or something." He grinned. "Don't worry so much."

They hauled their breakfast over to the counter and spread it out before the woman. "I don't suppose you take credit cards...?" Gray said.

The woman grunted. "You from the mainland?" she asked. Her hair hung like rope, hiding her eyes.

Polunu answered for him. "Yeah, but he ain't so bad."

"Cash only," the woman said.

Gray reached for his wallet, but Polunu held out his hand. "I got this one. You drove."

"Okay, thanks," Gray said, nodding. "I lost eight years of my life to the horror of driving up the world's most terrifying cliffs, but the world's lamest fruit salad is about to make it all worthwhile."

Polunu laughed as he fished a few dollars out of his pocket. He counted them out and made small talk with the owner. "You Auntie Alina?"

The woman nodded once. "Mm."

"Thank you for the food, auntie."

"Thank you for your money, cousin," she said, reaching for the bills.

"*He mea iki*, auntie. Hey, listen, you see any wild pigs around here lately? Maybe the last day or so?"

The woman paused. "Why do you ask me that?"

"We are pig hunters!" Polunu gave her a broad smile, and he thumped Gray in the chest, sending him wheeling back a few steps. "Two strong men, out hunting wild pigs!"

"You do not look like hunters to me."

"Today, we are," Polunu said proudly. "We search for a big *pua'a* today, auntie. You seen any run this way?"

The woman clapped her hand down over the dollar bills and slid them to her side of the counter. Her hair swung in front of her face, but she did not push it aside. When she spoke next, her voice took on a hard edge. "Do you seek Kamapua'a, children?"

Gray started at the sound of the pig-god's name. He leaned forward on the counter. "Is he near here? Do you know?"

"I know, mainlander," the woman breathed, her voice rattling. "I know."

Gray breathed a sigh of relief. "That's great!" He turned to Polunu. "Can you believe that? Talk about luck! Ma'am, can you tell us where we can—"

The woman raised her free hand, and even in the darkness, the shape of a knife blade was impossible to mistake. She stabbed the knife down at Gray's hand, but he yanked it back just as she drove the point down into the wood where his fingers had been a split second before. "What the hell!" he cried.

The woman ripped the knife from the wood and climbed up onto the counter, snarling and spitting. She swung the blade at Polunu, and he tumbled backward, but not fast enough; the knife sliced through his shirt and drew a thin line of blood across his belly. He yelped as he fell into the shelves behind him, cracking them in half, sending splinters and slowly rotting fruit scattering across the floor.

The woman scrambled off the counter, her long, tattered dress hanging limply from her skeletal frame. She swung her knife at Gray as he shrank back. Then she lunged, driving the knife at his chest. He picked up one of the mango crates and threw it up like a shield. The old woman's fist tore through the flimsy wood, and her knife exploded into the mess of mangos, sending orange, pulpy juice spattering across Gray's torso. Her wrist squirmed, the dripping point of the knife swiping in short, vicious circles. But the woman was up to her shoulder in the wooden bottom of the crate, and she could push her arm through no further. Gray's heart was just out of reach.

"*This is not okay!*" Gray cried. He shoved the crate hard, and the corner caught the woman in the jaw. She jerked backward, taking the wooden box with her. Gray ran to Polunu, who sat dazed against the wall, and tried to haul him to his feet. "Come on, come on, *come on!*" he yelled. But Polunu had slammed his head against one of the shelves in his fall, and a small trail of blood ran down his ear, pooling in the hollow of his collarbone and spreading like a blossom through the cotton of his shirt. His eyes rolled slowly up at his friend, clouded with confusion.

"What—?" was all he managed to say before the woman ripped her arm from the mango crate and flung herself onto Polunu, stabbing down at his belly with the knife. Gray shot his hand out and grabbed her by the wrist. The woman was surprisingly strong, and he had to hold her back with both hands. Her hair swung angrily and brushed across the big Hawai'ian's face as she struggled. Gray grunted with the strain of holding the old woman back, and he threw his shoulder into her arm. The force sent her flying off of Polunu and skidding across the floor, dragging Gray behind her.

The knife went spinning across the shack and out the door into the muddy gravel. Gray scrambled to his feet, and the woman leapt up too. She spun around, her hair flying up to reveal her face.

Gray screamed. Then he fell to his knees and threw up.

The old woman didn't *have* a face.

There were sunken divots where her eyes should have been, and a pinched ridge where her lips were supposed to be. Her skin was smooth and pulled taught over her blank skull.

"The full moon belongs to Kamapua'a," the faceless old woman hissed.

Gray had no idea where her voice was coming from, and it made his stomach lurch again. He fell down on his hands and pressed his forehead against the wood, desperate to make the room stop spinning. The old woman planted her feet on either side of his shaking shoulders. She grabbed a fistful of his hair and yanked his head up. She brought her blank face close to his ear and brushed her smooth skin against his cheek. He closed his eyes and tried to squirm away, but she held firm. "I will peel your skin and roast it over flames until it crackles, mainlander. I will taste your salt, your blood. You are nothing but rot and food for the *mujina* Alina." She wrapped her free hand around his chin and doubled her grip on the back of his head. With a grunt, she twisted his neck.

He heard a crack.

Then there was a thud as the old woman fell face-first to the floor. Gray peeled open his left eye. He saw the back of her head, a slow trickle of blood pooling out of her skull and mingling with the puddle of his vomit. He opened his right eye and rolled his head to look up. Polunu stood over both of them, holding a piece of the shattered wooden shelf in his hand. The crack Gray heard hadn't been his neck; it had been the old woman's head when Polunu hit it with the plank.

"Am I dead?" Gray whispered.

"Not yet," Polunu said. He reached down and hauled Gray up by the arm. The big man swayed a bit and put his hand on the wall for support. The two men stood quietly for some time, taking deep breaths and shaking reality back into their heads.

Finally, Gray pointed at the old woman and asked, "What the hell *is* that?"

"That," Polunu said, nudging the fallen woman with his toe, "is a *mujina*."

"I ask again," Gray said, rubbing his stomach and trying to keep it calm, "what the hell *is* that?"

"It's sort of...like a faceless witch."

"I thought you didn't have witches here," Gray frowned.

"Well, not *really* a witch. Just sort of...*our* version of witch. You know? Very powerful. Very mean."

"No kidding." Gray walked in a wide circle around the *mujina*, peeking at the horror of her featureless face from afar. "Is she dead?"

"I don't think so. It's very hard to kill a *mujina*. They got, like, demon strength."

"What should we do with her?" Gray asked.

Polunu shrugged. "What you do with witches on the mainland? You burn them, yeah?"

"Yeah," Gray said, rolling his eyes, "when it's the year 1784."

"Well, you wanna light her up?"

Gray blenched. "No. Not really."

"She's not a human," Polunu pointed out. "It wouldn't be murder, you know? She's an evil spirit."

"Then I don't want her haunting me when she's *actually* dead."

Polunu nodded. "Good point. What do we do with her, then?"

Gray glanced around the roadside shack. Out the back window, he saw a small grove of fruit trees and a few strips of farmed earth where a handful of scrawny pineapple plants were growing. Leaning up against one of the trees was an iron rake and a shovel.

"Well...I have sort of a terrible idea."

The rain had stopped, and it took less than an hour to bury the *mujina* up to her neck in the dirt. She only regained consciousness once during the process, right after they had dragged her out of the shack and stuck her feet in the hole. She came to as they were lowering her down by her shoulders, and she began to struggle, whipping her powerful arms and screaming at them in Hawai'ian. Polunu let go, and she hit the bottom hard. She tried to claw her way out, but Polunu hefted the shovel and clocked her over the head until she fell silent once more.

"She's going to have serious brain trauma," Gray pointed out with a frown.

"She was gonna roast your skin over fire and taste your salt," Polunu reminded him.

"Yeah. That's true. I guess if I'm being honest, I really don't care too much about her brain."

And now, as they tamped the soil back into place around her neck, her head began to bob, and she awoke once more. She struggled, but the weight of the earth held her still. "Release me!" she screamed from her non-mouth, her voice guttural and shaking with fury. "I will curse you so that your children are born with rotting skin and your grandchildren thirst for the blood of goats! Your fingers will shrivel into claws of bone, and your heads will shrink until your skull bursts through your skin and rips your flesh from your face! The beasts of Kanaloa will find you and unzip your skin and peel your flesh from your skeleton and string it through infinite fields of nettles and thorns! I will pull your nails from your toes with glowing hot tongs and stab them through your eyes so they bleed milk onto your tongue! Your kneecaps will be ripped from their sockets and ground into bread!"

Gray shook his head wearily and trotted back into the shack, picked up a crate full of mangos, emptied it out, brought it back outside, and placed it like a cage over the *mujina*'s head. Her curses became muffled and dim. Gray stepped back and crossed his arms proudly.

"Guess that's that," he said.

Polunu shrugged. "Guess so."

They headed back into the shack, picked up some of the scattered fruit, and had a quick second breakfast. "What now?" Gray asked, forcing down a last bite of souring mango and stepping out into the parking lot. "If we're being attacked by faceless witches, that's probably actually a *good* sign, right?"

Polunu nodded thoughtfully. "Not surprising Kamapua'a would put obstacles in our way. But it means he ain't taking no chances. We on the right track, all right. And it's gonna be a dangerous road."

"Yeah. I'm starting to think we should've asked the all-powerful *akua* for more than just a fish hook."

"Like what?"

"Like, I don't know. A demon-proof vest?"

"Aw, come on, cuz," Polunu grinned. "Where's the fun in that?"

Gray put his hands on his hips and raised his eyes to the steep green mountain that rose sharply behind Auntie Alina's. "You think she's up there?"

"Hi'iaka?" he asked. Gray nodded. "I don't know, brah. What does your heart tell you?"

"My heart tells me I should have stayed in St. Louis."

"Nah. That's stupid. 'Cause then we wouldn't be best friends, you know?"

"Best friends?" Gray asked, raising an eyebrow uncertainly.

"And your life, it would still be boring and sad."

"Um, my life was not boring and sad."

"It was definitely sad."

"It's just been sad *recently.*"

"And you seemed pretty boring at first, too. I think you were probably both boring and sad."

"Wow. Some best friend you are."

"Best friends always tell the truth," Polunu said, pleased. "Now you ask your heart: is your girl Hi'iaka up in *nā pali*?" He nodded toward the cliffs that stretched thousands of feet into the sky.

Gray breathed deeply. The mountain smelled of gardenia and dirt. The land was still slick with rain, and a strong must coated the air, weighing it down with a heavy wetness. He closed his eyes and slowed his breath. He reached out to Hi'iaka with his mind, letting his thoughts wander up the slope, searching for her among the hills. But he didn't feel her reach back. "I don't know," he sighed. "This is stupid. I can't—"

But just then, the wind changed. It blew down from the mountain, and it carried the unmistakable scent of vanilla and coconut.

Gray opened his eyes. "Whoa," he whispered, his heart thrumming. "She *is* up there! I can't believe that just—I mean, I just smelled her! Like, in a *good* way! Is that insane? She's up there. I really think she's up there!"

Polunu nodded. "Yeah. I know," he said.

"What do you mean, you know?"

"I saw wild boar tracks out back, past the pineapple plants, heading up into the hills. Way more tracks than normal. Like two whole herds, you know? Kamapua'a is definitely up there."

Gray sputtered. "Then why did you have me reach out with my stupid heart and feel to see if this was the right place?!" he demanded, suddenly feeling incredibly foolish.

"I just wanna prove that you got a serious crush, brah." He slapped Gray on the shoulder and grinned. "And now we know, yeah?"

"I'm gonna bury you next to the witch," Gray muttered, walking back toward the car.

"Hey, where you going, *haole*? We walk from here."

"Yeah, I figured that," Gray said, pulling open the back door. He reached in and pulled out Manaiakalani. Even in the dreary light, the great hook seemed to gleam. "But we're probably gonna need this, huh?"

"Ooooh, yeah, that's good thinking," Polunu nodded. "We should definitely bring the one thing that can actually hurt the pig-god."

"You're carrying it," Gray said, shoving the curved piece of bone against Polunu's chest. "Try not to lose it."

"You got it, brah. Let's go find the love of your life."

# Chapter 13

Kamapua'a stood outside the rusty shed and whispered to the trees.

Hi'iaka sat in the center of her little circle, her knees drawn up to her chin. Her dress was stained and filthy with rainwater and mud, and her bare feet were caked with dirt. She was not used to confinement of any sort, and her enslavement to the circle was a torture in itself. As she sat and stared at the pig-god hissing at his kukui trees, she imagined all the ways she would make him suffer when she broke free of the circle and took her revenge.

*If* she broke free of the circle. *If* she took her revenge.

It was the day of the full moon; the *mahina* would shine as a complete circle in the night sky, and by midnight, Hi'iaka's plight would be over, one way or the other.

How Kamapua'a would manage to steal her *mana* from her shadow—or even *if* he would steal her *mana* from her shadow—was still a mystery...but though the pig-god could be quick-tempered and mindlessly brutal, he was not a stupid creature, and though Hi'iaka showed him a stoic face, she felt a tremor of fear in her heart. If the Lord of Pigs said he could steal her energy, her power, then it was very possible that he had found a way. The Hawai'ian chiefs of old believed that if another man stepped into his

shadow, that man would steal his *mana*, and so it became true because it was so firmly believed. But the idea of stealing the *mana* of
a god...this was unheard of, and if Kamapua'a had devised a method
of draining *nā akua*, then there would be no limit to the power he
could accumulate from the old gods of Hawai'i. He would become
one of the few truly unstoppable forces in the universe. He would
become as powerful as time and as unyielding as death.

He had to be stopped. Not just for Hi'iaka's sake, but for the
sake of all Hawai'i—and maybe the entire world. She prayed that
Grayson had received her message. He wasn't her first choice; he
was sweet, and he was kind, and she had stayed on the island of
Maui in the hopes of seeing him again, yes, but he was not equipped
to do battle with the gods. Trapped in her circle, though, her power
was weak, and she could only send her spirit out to those keeping
her close to their hearts at that moment. Pele had not been dwelling
on her little sister; neither had Haumea, her mother, or Kāne, her
father. There had only been Grayson Park, standing alone on his
hotel deck and aching for her in his chest. That is how she was able
to send him the message through the crabs. She only hoped that he
had seen the words...that he had somehow managed to find her sister, that Pele had raised an army capable of fighting a demigod, that
Grayson was leading them here, right now, to storm the compound
and defeat the sinister pig-god.

It was much to ask of a sad and clumsy mortal from the Midwest. She did not have much hope.

But she did have *some* hope. Because she decided she *must* have
some hope.

What else was left for her?

Kamapua'a began screaming at the kukui trees, drawing Hi'iaka from her thoughts. The trees rustled in the wind and bent their

branches to whisper in the pig-god's ear, and he was greatly angered by what he heard. He spat on the trees and cursed them before storming back into the shack.

He removed his boar face as he approached his prisoner, appearing once again as the handsome human with shining black hair. "Well," he said, giving her a small smile that did little to hide his anger, "it seems you were right, Little Egg. Your sister sent a warrior."

"Of course she did," Hi'iaka said, relief washing through her chest. She smiled up at the demigod from her seat on the muddy floor. "You could not think she would let you take her sweet sister and not send a warrior to lead an army to set me free."

"An army, is it?" the pig-god said, and he began pacing slowly around the circle, stalking Hi'iaka like prey. "What sort of army enlists only two?"

"Two?" Hi'iaka said. Her breath caught in her throat, but she fought to retain her composure. "What two are those?"

"My trees tell me we are being sieged by a *haole* and a *kohola*...a whale that walks like a man. Is this your sister's army, Little Egg?"

"Call me Little Egg again, and I will break you like a shell," she said between clenched teeth.

Kamapua'a smiled. "Yes, wouldn't that be something?"

"My sister need not send a legion," Hi'iaka continued, struggling to sound fierce in the face of a sinking heart. "If she sent two warriors, then they are the only two warriors needed to defeat a semi-god like Kamapua'a."

The Lord of Pigs flushed dark red. He gritted his teeth. "It seems they are not without some skill," he conceded, his jaw tight. The upturned canines of his lower jaw grew longer, poking out from between his lips. He took a deep breath and managed to keep his animal face subdued. "The kukui say they have bested my *mujina*."

"Perhaps the *haole* carries with him some mainlander magic," she said. "I see your face starting to slip, pig-god. Do not be ashamed; it is natural to fear what you do not understand. And I think there is *much* that you do not understand."

"Alina was weak," Kamapua'a spat. "They have spared her, but where they failed in that, I will succeed. She will be punished; she will not live through the night. But neither will your army of two. And neither will you yourself...Little Egg."

Hi'iaka seethed. "I warned you, demi-pig: you will break before the day is out."

But Kamapua'a was not listening. He whistled through his teeth, and Hi'iaka heard a low rumble in the distance. The pig-god stood at the entrance to the shack, his fists planted on his hips, waiting. The rumbling grew louder, and the ground began to shake. A stampede of boars flooded into the shack. They grunted and rutted excitedly, nudging each other with their tusks and slamming their rumps together. Kamapua'a raised his hands into the air, and the hogs quieted down. Three pigs, the three biggest, stepped forward from the pack. Each one had a large, round rock in its mouth, like a great stone egg. The first pig bowed its head and laid its stone at Kamapua'a's feet. The second pig set its stone next to the first, and the third set its stone down in turn. Then the pigs backed away, pushing the others out to form a semi-circle around the demigod.

Kamapua'a crouched down above the three stones. He let his human face wash away, leaving the fierce boar's head in its place. He lifted the first stone to his mouth and crushed it between his teeth. It cracked in half like an egg. He placed the broken stone back on the ground, and out slithered a fat lizard, green with shimmering purple diamonds spattered across its back. The lizard reared up onto its hind legs and stood at attention before the pig-lord. Then Kamapuaʻa picked up the second stone and bit it in half, and out stalked a thin, gaunt lizard, with brown scales and yellow slashes across its back. It, too, stood before Kamapuaʻa, who picked up the third stone and released a strong, hulking lizard, dark green with blue and yellow dots across its back and head, and two short, spiky horns thrusting out from its brow.

"*Moʻo*," Hiʻiaka breathed. A great chill ran through her. It had been centuries since she had last seen—or even heard rumor of—a shape-shifting lizard demon on the island. She had thought them extinct. Kakmapuaʻa must have gone to great lengths to mine these three from their slumber in the rocks far beneath the earth. And now Hiʻiaka's blood ran cold, for she knew the great and terrible power of the *moʻo*.

*I have killed Grayson*, she thought, trembling. *I have led him to his death.*

Kamapuaʻa must have guessed at her secret sadness, for he gave her a drooling, wolfish grin. He snorted once, twice, three times through his powerful snout. The three lizards bowed low to Kamapuaʻa, and he returned their bows, digging his tusks through the muddy ground. Then he whispered to the lizards in a series of squeals and grunts too low for Hiʻiaka to hear. They bobbed their heads in understanding, and in agreement, and then they ran off, scattering through the jungle and disappearing into the brush.

Kamapuaʻa rose to his full height and snorted at his prisoner. The other boars squealed with victory. "That should take care of

Pele's army," the pig-god snipped. "Now we can hold our moonlight ritual without interruption."

Hi'iaka's heart sank, and she began to cry, for she knew that the Lord of Pigs was right.

# Chapter 14

Gray was having a heart attack.

"I'm having a heart attack!" he cried, wheezing and clutching his chest. "I'm really having a heart attack!"

"Does your left arm feel weird?" Polunu asked.

Gray shook out his arm. He flexed his fingers a few times. He didn't feel anything strange. "No."

"Then you ain't having a heart attack, cousin. You just *really* out of shape."

There was no real trail to speak of heading up the mountain, and they had to tramp down the brush as they followed the uneven path of the pigs. The climb, along with the stamping down of plants and the pushing aside of branches, had Gray winded before they'd gone 500 feet. "How much further, you think?" he asked, stopping to catch his breath.

"You serious? We, like, just started, *haole*. Dang. You gonna die on me?"

"How is it possible," Gray wheezed, "that you're hardly even breaking a sweat? I mean, look at you." He gestured wildly at the Hawai'ian's general chubbiness.

Polunu gave Manaiakalani a few practice swings, something he did every few steps, just to get used to the feel of the hook in his hand. "I think that says more about you than it does about me," he pointed out.

Gray shook his head. "I have got to get a gym membership," he decided. "This is it. This is the year."

Before long, they heard the sound of rushing water roaring somewhere off through the woods to their right. "Is that a river?" Gray asked. "Maybe we should follow it." He took a few steps off the path, toward the sound of the water.

"Hey, hold on! Why you wanna follow a river? This pig path will go right to Kamapua'a, cuz."

"Do pigs go in straight lines?" Gray crossed his arms.

"Well." Polunu blinked. He looked up at the trampled grass that wound its way up the hillside. "No. It doesn't look like it."

"Water does. So let's just follow that."

But Polunu was adamant. "No way. It's safer to follow the pigs. The rains can come any time in the upcountry, and that river can flood like lightning. You don't want to be caught in that. We should stick to the pigs."

"You know what happens when you follow a herd of wild boars?" Gray asked.

Polunu shrugged.

"Eventually, you find them. And when that happens, it's going to be two of us against who knows how many razor-toothed wild animals. I think we should follow the water."

"Water is more dangerous," Polunu insisted. "You get caught in the falls, you get drowned, crushed, and swept into the ocean like *that*." He tried to snap his fingers, but they were too clumsy. He frowned. "You know," he clarified, "real quick."

"You know how fast a wild boar will eat you?" He snapped his fingers, twice, just to emphasize how easily he could do it. "Like *that*," he said smugly. In truth, he had no idea how brutal the pigs might be, but he had a vague understanding that wild boars were generally thought to be dangerous. And, truth be told, he didn't particularly care about following the water, but since his view of the world was in the process of spinning completely upside-down, he just wanted to feel like he was in control of *something*, even if it was just the path they took.

"I'm tellin' you, brah. The safest way is—" But before he could finish the sentence, they heard a heavy rustling in the undergrowth. Polunu grabbed Gray by the collar and yanked him behind a tree. "Shhh!" he said, holding a finger to his lips. He peeked around the tree. Gray squirmed loose and looked back, too. They saw leaves shaking near the pig path. The hidden thing was coming closer.

Gray nodded down at Manaiakalani. Polunu's brow creased in confusion. Gray nodded more pointedly. Polunu creased his forehead harder. "Oh, for the love of—the hook! Use the hook! Stab the thing!"

"We don't even know what *the thing* is!"

"We know it's not either of us, and so far, the only other things we know for sure are out here besides us are wild boars, demigods who want us dead, and witches who don't even have a face!" Gray hissed.

"Just wait and see," Polunu insisted.

They didn't have to wait long. The rustling grew closer. Soon it seemed like the leaves all around them were trembling. Gray swore that he could hear the low growl of some fanged beast. He whimpered in terror and threw his arms over his eyes as the monster leapt out from the grass.

It was a fat little lizard, green with a gleaming pattern of purple diamond-shaped scales stamped across its back.

"You can relax, auntie," Polunu sighed. "It's just a lizard."

Gray peeked out from behind his arms and exhaled when he saw the little creature blinking up at them from the ground. "Don't call me auntie," he said, slapping Polunu's arm with the back of his hand. "I thought it was a wolf."

Polunu laughed. "There ain't no wolves in Hawai'i," he said, twirling Maui's hook by the grip. "There ain't no predators of any kind."

"Oh. Wait, seriously?"

"Seriously."

"Well that's something you could have told me earlier."

"I could have," Polunu grinned, "but I wanted to see if you'd wet yourself again."

"I never wetted myself!" Gray cried, mortified.

"Tell that to the front of your pants, brah. Pele sure scared the piss out of you." He roared with laughter.

Gray glowered, his face turning as red as Maui dirt. "It is *not* funny," he said. "She threw lava at me."

"Yeah, I know, that *was* pretty scary," Polunu admitted. Then he laughed. "Almost as scary as this lizard!"

"I hate you. Shut up." Gray looked down at the lizard. The lizard stared back up at him, flicking out its tongue. "Why is it staring at me?" he asked.

"Maybe she likes you," Polunu said, laughing so hard now that he had to put a hand on the tree for support. "Maybe you have a new fiancée!"

But Gray was too caught up in the strangeness of the little lizard to process Polunu's words. "No, seriously. Look at it." He moved to the left; the lizard scuttled to the left, too. Gray moved to the right;

the lizard scrambled to follow. Gray took two steps back; the lizard scurried forward. Gray took two steps forward; the lizard stayed right where it was, less than three feet from Gray's toes now.

Polunu stopped laughing as he watched this strange ballet. He frowned down at the lizard. He tilted his head to the side, as if the creature were familiar to him somehow, but he couldn't quite place it...

Then the lizard reared up on its back legs and spread its front claws wide. It opened its mouth and hissed.

Suddenly, everything clicked for Polunu.

He rammed his shoulder forward, knocking Gray to the ground just as the lizard lunged. It dove forward and swiped Polunu's arm, drawing a thin line of blood beneath his web of tattoos. Polunu and Gray went tumbling head-over-heels into the brush. The lizard hit the ground and rolled. Then it expanded and stretched, and when it leapt back up to its hind legs, it had quadrupled in size.

Gray grabbed a nearby tree and pulled himself to his feet. "What *is* that?" he cried, stabbing a finger toward the lizard that was now the size of a small dog.

"A *mo'o!*" Polunu shouted. "Run!" He grabbed Gray's wrist and pulled him up toward the pig trail. The lizard fell back down to all fours, and something rattled in the back of its throat. Gray chanced a look over his shoulder as they ran, and he saw the lizard push its claws into the earth, sinking deeper and deeper until the soil was all way up to its shoulders.

"It's doing something weird!" Gray cried as they pushed through the jungle.

"Don't look back!" Polunu yelled. "Just *go!*"

A wild mango tree upended itself in their path, crashing to the ground and blocking their way. The two men skidded to a stop. Polunu tried to go left, but another tree fell in that direction, quaking the earth and blocking that route, too. They ran back to the right, and the dirt thrust itself up into a high wall. Polunu leapt up, but even with his great height, he couldn't reach the flat ledge of earth.

"What the hell is happening?!" Gray screamed.

But in the end, he didn't need Polunu to answer. He looked back down the hill the way they had come, the only way still open to them. He saw the lizard with its claws sunken into the earth, and he noticed the creature's subtle movements. Its left arm quivered, and the tree on the left began to shake. It rolled itself toward them, end over end, driving them back toward the dirt wall. Then the lizard worked its right arm, and the dirt wall began to curve at the top like an ocean wave. It curled over them, and bits of soil began to rain down.

The lizard was controlling nature.

"Run!" Polunu yelled. He threw himself over the trunk of the felled mango tree, hitting the ground hard on the other side. Maui's hook went skittering off into the trees. Polunu struggled to his feet and motioned frantically for Gray to follow. Gray tried, but he slipped on his first step, and before he could reach the tree, the wave of dirt crashed down on him, slamming him into the ground and pinning him beneath its crushing weight.

Gray gasped for breath, a mouthful of soil clogging his throat. He sucked the dirt into his lungs, choking and sputtering. He felt the veins on his neck start to pulse through his skin, and he hacked up as much soil as he could, but he was stuck in the earth, unable to move, and for every breath out, he sucked another dusty breath in. Tears stung at his eyes as his face began to turn purple.

Polunu leapt back over the tree trunk, but the tree flung itself back upright as he crossed over, catching the big Hawai'ian and throwing him across the jungle. He crashed into a rainbow euca-lyptus a few dozen yards away and thudded to the ground, the wind knocked out of his sails.

Tiny black squares began to swarm through Gray's vision. He struggled with his arms, shrugged with his shoulders, but the dirt was too heavy, and he was trapped. Then he felt the smallest bit of pressure on his back, pressing down through the earth, and he shuddered, because he knew what that pressure was.

The lizard had come to finish him off.

*So stupid*, Gray thought as the darkness began to spread through his whole body. *Death by lizard. So, so stupid.*

The *mo'o* crawled over his shoulders and around his head. It planted itself in front of his face and bared its sharp teeth with a hiss. It stuck its claws into the dirt and began to pull them close to-gether through the earth. Gray felt the dirt on either side of his ribs begin to compress. What little breath he had was being squeezed out of his lungs. He winced as he heard a rib pop, a dull, muffled sound through the dirt. The *mo'o* almost seemed to laugh, flicking its tongue between its teeth. The sight of it snapped something in Gray's brain. There was injury, and then there was adding *insult* to injury, and enough was enough. He drew what breath he could, worked together a glob of saliva on his tongue, and spat it directly into the big lizard's dumb, open mouth.

The *mo'o* reared back in surprise, pulling his claws from the dirt as he did. The pressure on Gray's ribs instantly relaxed. The dirt fell away, and he wriggled forward. The lizard demon choked on Gray's spit, shaking its head like a confused dog. Gray wiggled himself closer to freedom, pushing with his knees and grasping for purchase with his shoulders. He broke through the dirt, and his arms were finally able to burst free. The *mo'o* swallowed down his spit and lunged forward on its hind legs.

Gray scrambled forward, toward the mango tree.

The lizard sank its claws into his ankle, and he screamed. He felt a stream of blood instantly begin to trickle down his foot. He flopped over onto his back, knocking the lizard onto its side with his other foot. He reached blindly around him, not taking his eyes from the *mo'o*, and his fingers closed around a thick mango branch. He yanked hard, and the branch snapped and broke free in his hand. The *mo'o* righted itself and plunged its claws back into the dirt. Gray swung the branch, and just as the two fallen trees began to tremble and slide together, with him trapped between their trunks, he brought the tree limb down hard on the monster's head. It burst like a melon, strings of pink and red goo exploding in all directions, coating Gray's legs and splattering his shirt.

"Oh my God," he whispered, disgusted.

Polunu appeared from behind the mango tree, holding his side and wincing as he walked. "Nice job, *haole*! Gross, but...you know. Nice."

Gray rolled over and pushed himself up to his knees. "What the hell *was* that thing?" he asked, holding his sore ribs as he climbed up to a seat on the tree trunk.

"An evil lizard-god. A *mo'o*. I ain't never seen one in person before." He peered down at the headless body, with its arms buried in the dirt and its neck lying limp in a pool of blood.

"So I guess we're still on the right track," Gray said. He coughed, and a cloud of dirt puffed out of his mouth.

"I think maybe we got Kamapua'a scared," Polunu said, lumbering off into the woods to find Manaiakalani. "A *mujina* and a *mo'o*. That's a serious combination, brah. He ain't messin' around."

"Great. Can't wait to see what's next," Gray wheezed.

Polunu found the hook wrapped around an avocado tree a few yards away. He picked it up and dusted it off. "Should probably hold onto this tighter, huh?" he said, giving it a few swings through the air.

"I *told* you to stab it to death," Gray pointed out.

Polunu shrugged. "You were right. But hey, even a broken watch is right once a day," Polunu said.

"A broken watch is right *twice* a day."

Polunu laughed. "Not if it's *really* broken!"

Gray rolled his eyes. "Glad you've still got a sense of humor."

"Hey, we're still alive, you know?"

"And bleeding." Gray nodded at Polunu's arm. The blood flow had slowed, but it still oozed down his elbow.

"Bleeding is better than dead." He wiped the scratch against his shirt. It only smeared the blood. He frowned at the mess. Then he shrugged. "Oh well."

Gray tended to his own blood, pulling a handful of leaves from the mango tree and dabbing at his ankle. "I probably have rabies."

"No rabies in Hawai'i," Polunu said proudly.

"And I think I broke a rib," Gray continued, wincing through a breath.

"Nah. You break a rib, you *know* it. You probably just popped it out of place or something."

Gray sighed. "Yeah. I probably *just* popped it out of place." He wiped away the blood and tossed the leaves aside. Then he rested his elbows on his knees and let his head fall between his legs. "If we do make it to Hi'iaka, she better be damned well happy to see me."

"You gonna tell her you got a new fiancée?" Polunu grinned, lifting his eyebrows at the headless *mo'o*.

"There is something seriously wrong with you."

"Oh, plenty of things, braddah," the big man agreed, "plenty of things. Right now, the big thing is that's it's almost lunchtime, and we didn't pack no lunch."

"We just had second breakfast!"

"Yeah," Polunu said, tilting his head in confusion, "and now, it's time for lunch."

Gray frowned. Fighting lizard demons was apparently hungry work, because he felt his own stomach growling, too. "Yeah. Guess we probably should have grabbed more witch-fruit for the hike, huh?"

"It's okay. We got some good food right here."

Gray followed the Hawai'ian's gaze down toward the dead lizard and grimaced. His stomach lurched. "You don't mean—?"

Polunu gave him a wink. "I mean your tree, brah. Hand me a mango. They look pretty close to ripe."

# Chapter 15

Hi'iaka felt a cramp seize up in her leg. She pushed herself to her feet and shook out her ankle, turning it and turning it and trying to work away the pain.

Gray was as good as dead.

She had to get out of that circle.

It was such a simple thing, the thin ring drawn in the dirt. But it had been drawn by Kamapua'a himself with a little bit of magic and a great amount of strong, unbridled intention. And when it came to matters of the gods, intention was everything. It sealed her within its boundary; she was unable to step across the line unless the circle was broken. And she herself was powerless to break it.

Not that she hadn't tried. She'd attempted to rub through the dirt, but an invisible force stayed her hand. She had kicked earth onto the circle, but that, too, collided with an unseen barrier and collected in little piles on the inside of her cell. She was fully contained, and nothing she could do from the inside would smear the line and break the circle to set her free.

Help would have to come from the outside.

In addition to keeping her trapped, the pig-god's ring dulled her powers to almost nothing. But it could not extinguish her strength altogether. She closed her eyes and sent her spirit searching across the mountain, seeking a sorcerer of even modest ability. If she could find a practitioner of the old magic in the jungle, she could make a plea for help. Surely there was no sorcerer alive who would deny the call of Hawai'i's patron *akua*.

But magic was in short supply these days. The old ways were all but extinct. The signs were everywhere. The powerful hula of Hawai'i's past had been whittled down to luau shows for tourists; the tales of *nā akua* were fading from the memories of the aged and dying; ancient medicines were being replaced with modern pharmaceuticals; magic had withered and dried like lilikoi left in the sun. So she was not surprised when she felt no sorcerers on the mountain; her range was small, the circle kept her spirit weak, and magicians were not nearly as plentiful as they had once been.

She tried casting spells on the pigs, though she knew that they were imbued with Kamapua'a's own brand of magic. They belonged to him, and it would take great strength to peel away their loyalty to their demigod. She tried anyway. She bore into them with her eyes, searching, trying to penetrate their minds. She whispered the chants taught to her by the elder gods so many eons ago. The words flowed easily from her lips, and the air around her sparked with their power.

But the pigs did not succumb.

Hi'iaka sighed. She rubbed her wrists together slowly, an old habit that took her when she was lost in deep thought. She hardly noticed the dirt that swirled up around her feet when she did, matching the rotations of her wrists. If she could cast her spell on the dirt outside the ring, she could wipe away the line...but of course Kamapua'a knew that, and her bond with the land was of no use against his entrapments.

She closed her eyes and remembered with perfect clarity a time when all of Hawai'i would have risen to her call. When the tribes of man and even the land itself, the very sands of the beach and the birds in the trees, would have rallied themselves to her side. The ancient people knew how to pay homage to their *akua*. Kamapua'a would never have held her captive in the time of the Hawai'ian kings, he *could* not have. He would have been driven out with the united force of all the islands, great and small, and he would have drowned under the strength of her will.

But patron gods were for storybooks now. No one sought her favor anymore. No faithful believer laid *ho'okupu* at her feet. All of Hawai'i would have risen up to protect her once; now, a small bit of dust was all that could be bothered.

There was only one other trick for her to try. With her powers restrained, it was hardly worth the effort, but she could think of no other option: she would call the lightning, or she would fall to Kamapua'a's whim. Even with her full strength, the lightning was difficult to control. It was a wild, ferocious thing, and it tended to crackle and split where it would. The whole sky was the open domain of the lightning's electric fingers, and even at her full strength, she could not always ensure its direction. But she would do what she could to channel the raw power regardless and summon it to her aid.

She needed lightning born of a tempest. She closed her eyes and began to send what spirit she could through the invisible membrane of her circular cell. Her powers were weakened, but they had not been destroyed. Not yet.

She pushed her intention into the sky, and the clouds began to gather.

First, she would bring the rain.

And then, if she had any strength left, she would bring the storm.

# Chapter 16

"Great. And now it's starting to rain." Gray held out his hand. Little raindrops spattered his palm.

"The rain is good!" Polunu said. "Rain makes—"

"I know, I know. It makes the taro grow."

They had resumed their trek up the pig trail, Gray yielding to the greater wisdom of following a path already laid out for them. But even with the grass trampled down, the terrain was getting harder to push through. A few times, Polunu had to wield Maui's hook like a scythe, cutting down wild ferns and knocking their way clear. "*E kala mai ia'u,*" he whispered as the hook sliced through the bushes, cutting down their stalks. "*E kala mai ia'u.*"

"What's that mean?" Gray asked, wheezing up the hill.

"I'm asking the plants for forgiveness."

Gray stopped. He raised an eyebrow. "Seriously?"

"Sure. It's not the plants' fault we need to pass through and cut them down. It's *our* fault. It's okay, you know, they'll grow back, but it's good for them to know I'm sorry."

"I don't think they can hear you."

"The earth can always hear. We just do not always speak."

"Hmpf. Maybe the plants should speak to the pigs and ask them why they didn't trample a better path so we wouldn't have to cut down so many of their friends." Polunu let go of a branch he was holding back, and it swatted Gray in the face. "Hey!"

"Whoops." Polunu shrugged. "Sorry."

The leafy canopy overhead protected them from most of the rain, which began to fall harder. The sound of the droplets splashing against the leaves was soothing in its gentle, arrhythmic patter. The constant crush of the river began to grow louder over the din of rain, and after climbing for a few more minutes in silence, Polunu held up his hand for Gray to stop.

"What?" Gray asked, struggling up alongside the Hawai'ian. His breath was labored; he was still sort of choking on dirt that just wouldn't clear from his lungs.

But mostly, he was out of shape.

Polunu pointed through the branches. Gray craned his neck, but the growth was too thick. "I don't see anything," he said. He took a step forward and pushed through the trees. "What are you—?" Suddenly, the forest floor crumbled away from beneath his feet, and he was spinning over the edge of a two hundred foot drop into the basin of the river. He screamed and tried to scramble back from the edge, but his hiking shoes slipped in the wet earth and skidded out from under him. He pitched forward over the cliff.

Polunu snagged his arm just as he fell and yanked him back to safety.

"Holy hell!" Gray screamed. "I almost just *died*!" He thought for a second, and then added, *"Again!"*

"You making a habit of it today, *haole.*"

Gray shook his head, his eyes wide and disbelieving. He gestured out over the valley and the long, powerful waterfall that spilled the river down the side of the mountain. "I mean, that just came out of *nowhere*!"

"It's dangerous to climb where there's no good trail. You never know what you gonna find in the woods." Polunu turned to head back to a safer part of the hill, but he paused before they moved on. "Next time, when I say to stop, you should probably stop. You know?"

"You didn't say stop," Gray pointed out. "You just waved your hand. That could have meant anything."

"But it didn't mean anything. It meant 'stop.'"

"Duly noted. Thank you."

"*He mea 'ole.*"

Gray pushed back through the forest, following Polunu's steps. They climbed higher, keeping the roar of the waterfall far to their right as the vegetation began to change. Gray kept his eyes aimed intently down at his feet, determined not to take another wrong step, but when he noticed Manaiakalani making a new, almost hollow *thunk* against the brush, he looked up to see what Polunu was hacking away at. He lifted his eyes, and he gasped.

They had stumbled into a sprawling grove of bamboo.

"Whoa. This is crazy," Gray murmured in awe. The thick green stalks rose high into the sky, swaying in the breeze. The rain almost seemed to pop as it fell against the trunks of the ancient grass, some of which were thicker than his arm. A different type of plant, a small, creeping thing with heart-shaped leaves, clung close to the ground and carpeted the earth like a blanket, but the larger trees had all fallen away, and there was only bamboo stretching into the sky in every direction, as far as the eye could see, tall and thin and graceful. Gray reached out and ran his hand along the smooth joints of a particularly wide bamboo plant. "It's like walking through a Crate and Barrel," he whispered.

The bamboo provided less cover from the rain than the trees had; soon water was dripping from Gray's hair. The wetness of the earth burned to a haze in the upcountry heat, and a low mist covered the ground, wrapping its gauzy web around the bases of the bamboo plants. The entire grove took on a distinctly otherworldly appearance.

Polunu lowered Manaiakalani and began to sidestep through the bamboo instead of batting it away. His big belly pushed the green stalks to the side; when he passed through, they swayed back, knocking into their neighbors and sounding out a crisp, hollow tone and playing a strange, serene, tribal tattoo high above their heads.

"I can't see the pig trail," Gray realized, searching the bamboo forest with his eyes. "Where'd they go?"

"Even the wild animals know this is a sacred and special place," Polunu said, wedging his way through the trees. "You can see the hoof prints in the mud, though, yeah? They came through, but they went slow. They don't wanna disturb the bamboo."

"It's incredible," Gray murmured.

Polunu smiled. "It's home," he said proudly.

Then something in the jungle went *crunch*, and both men dropped into a crouch.

"What was that?"

"Don't know," Polunu whispered. "Sounded like someone coming this way."

"Stab it!" Gray hissed.

Polunu tightened his grip on Manaiakalani and held it up at his side. Gray tried to flatten himself against a stalk of bamboo, which was absurd, since he was wider than a broomstick. He pushed the rain-soaked hair out of his eyes and held his breath, while Polunu wielded the hook. The footsteps crunched closer.

And then the intruder was upon them.

"Oh," Polunu said, straightening up and blushing a little from embarrassment when the stranger came into view among the bamboo stalks. "*Aloha.*"

It was an old man, feeble and frail, with long, ropy muscles straining against his tautly drawn skin. His white hair clung to his skull in thin wisps; his squinting eyes were sunken above a small, squarish nose. He wore simple, rough-spun clothing; his pant legs were stained red with Maui dirt, and his shirt had been woven for a much larger man. He wore a rag tied around his neck, damp with rain and sweat. Each hand held a big wooden bucket, filled nearly to the brim with water from the river. His hands shook as he wove his way through the bamboo, and water sloshed over the rims of the buckets, splashing to the ground.

"*Aloha,*" the old man replied, his voice creaking like a weathervane. It didn't sound like he used it very often. He eyed the pair of men mistrustfully and adjusted his route, veering further away from them as he passed.

"Can we help you, uncle?" Polunu asked.

"Polunu," Gray whispered. There was something unnerving about coming across another soul in this misty bamboo grove, even if it was a frail, elderly man. Gray was about to raise an objection, but Polunu waved him off.

The old man grunted as he eased his buckets down to the ground. He straightened up and untied the rag from around his neck. He mopped it against his forehead, then rolled it up and tied it once more around his throat. "Not going far," he finally answered.

He dipped his hand into one of the buckets and lifted a palm full of water to his lips. "*Mahalo*, Lono; *mahalo*, Nāmaka," he murmured, shaking the water from his fingers.

Polunu tucked Manaiakalani under his arm and strode up to the old man. "If it ain't far to go, then we ain't got far to help," he said cheerfully. "Come on, *haole*," he said, nodding toward the other bucket. "Help our uncle."

Gray stepped forward uneasily, making a wide berth around the old man, who watched him sharply from behind his heavy, wrinkled lids. They didn't break eye contact, even when Gray plowed into a thick piece of bamboo and smashed his nose on the hard stalk.

"Don't be so weird," Polunu said, shaking his head. He hefted his water bucket easily and began walking in the direction the old man had been heading. "This way, uncle?" he called.

The old man nodded slowly, not taking his eyes off of Gray. "Not far," he said again through thin, unsmiling lips. His face streamed with thin trails of falling rain, but he did not flinch from the feel of it. "Not very far."

Gray reached down and fumbled for the handle of the bucket. He finally had to take his eyes off the old man so he could see where he was grabbing. He only looked down for one breath, but when he raised his head again, the old man had moved ten feet closer, standing just at Gray's elbow. Gray yelped in surprise, and a small tidal wave of water sloshed out over the edge of the bucket.

"Careful!" Polunu chided, clucking his tongue.

"Sorry," Gray replied. The old man didn't say a word; he simply stared at the mainlander with narrow, unblinking eyes. "Sorry," Gray said again, this time to the old man.

He gestured after Polunu. "Not far," he repeated.

"Yeah, I got it," Gray muttered, carefully turning his back on the old man and following after his friend. "Not far, not far, we're not going far."

They hauled the water up the hill, balancing the buckets carefully and trying not to spill it all. The rain fell harder, creating hundreds of little ripples in the buckets and adding to the volume, which made Gray feel a little less bad about the water he'd already spilled.

As they continued up through the bamboo forest, the ground became wetter, more slippery, and Gray's hiking shoes had a hard time finding purchase in the mud. He nearly fell more than once, only barely catching himself on the bamboo before falling to his knees. Polunu didn't seem to be having much better luck; he stopped every few yards to adjust his feet inside his old flip-flops and investigate the ground for the best footing forward.

And Gray didn't know if it was the terrain or the rain or the altitude, but the bucket felt like it was getting heavier with every step. When he'd first picked it up, it weighed maybe ten pounds, but as he struggled up the hill, it had grown to thirty pounds now, at least, and it was getting heavier. He had to grab the handle with two hands, and even then, he wasn't able to hold the bucket above the mud. Soon he had no choice but to drag the bucket along the ground, tilted up at an incline so he wouldn't spill too much of its contents.

And he was so *tired*—not just exhausted from the strain of carrying the bucket, but a sleepy sort of tired that he just couldn't shake. He could barely keep his eyes open. He'd only had one cup of coffee before leaving the hotel instead of his usual three or four, and that had been an obvious mistake, but still. He shouldn't have been *this* tired. His eyes were as dry as cotton, and his head kept drooping low. The fight to stay awake was suddenly all-consuming. "I can't…I need…a break," he whispered, letting the bucket fall from his hands. It crashed onto the ground and toppled onto its side, rolling back down the hill and spilling water everywhere. Gray's vision went soft as his lids lowered themselves over his eyes. He sank to his knees, and he looked up through the bamboo, wanting to call out to Polunu, but he was too tired to speak…and besides, Polunu was already lying down in the mud, snoring softly against a cluster of bamboo. Gray rolled over onto his back and began to breathe deeply, letting sleep take him.

The last thing he saw was the old man standing over him, staring down through the rain and licking his lips with a thin, forked tongue.

# Chapter 17

When Gray came to, the rain was still falling, and his hands were tied behind his back.

"No," he moaned, shaking the sleep from his head and twisting his wrists, straining at the rope that bound him to a strong bamboo plant. "No, no, no!"

"I'm sorry, cuz," Polunu said. He was propped up against an especially thick stalk of bamboo, his hands tied similarly. Tears streamed down his face, mixing with the rain that soaked his shirt. There was no sign of Manaiakalani. "This one's on me."

Gray smelled smoke. He sniffed at the air; the scent was unmistakable. He turned his head, trying to find the source of it, but all he could see was bamboo in every direction, towering over the lower leafy plants. He twisted awkwardly onto his side and craned his head backward over his shoulder. From that uncomfortable angle, he could see the old man standing in a clearing, crouched low over a small pile of damp wood, blowing onto the ghostly flames that flickered against the drying grass beneath the sticks. Maui's hook lay in the mud on the far side of the logs. "What's he doing?" Gray whispered, trying not to draw the attention of the old man.

"I think he's starting a fire," Polunu moaned.

Gray rolled his eyes. "No kidding. *Why* is he starting a fire?"

"Only two reasons to start a fire in the woods; heat yourself, or heat your food."

"But it's, like, 80 degrees out here," Gray said. He stopped. He thought. "Wait, you think he wants to *eat* us?!" he hissed. Polunu shrugged sadly. "What about a third option? There's got to be a third option! Right? Keeping animals away! People start fires to keep animals away! Right?"

"We got no predators in Hawai'i," Polunu reminded him.

"Oh yeah," Gray said. He blinked. "Well, shit."

The old man's fire grew as the wood began to smoke. Soon, flames danced along the branches, and the man threw more logs on the fire.

"What do we do?" Gray whispered, struggling against his bonds. The rope was tied with a thick knot, and there was no chance of pulling it loose.

Polunu was struggling with his ropes, too.

"Don't be big for nothing," Gray pleaded. "Please, please, please tear through that rope."

Polunu didn't reply. He simply nodded through his grunts.

The fire at their backs continued to grow in size and intensity. Soon, the mist of the rain paled in comparison to the heavy white smoke that drifted through the bamboo. It stung Gray's eyes and tickled his lungs. He began to cough, and after vomiting twice, choking on dirt, and now inhaling huge plumes of wood smoke, his raw throat was burning with its own fire.

He fell back to his side, trying to keep below the smoke. The fire blazed brightly, even in the cloudy light. The rain came down in diagonal slashes, and the logs sputtered and hissed as the drops fell. The old man loosed the rag from his neck and pulled his shirt up over his head.

Gray gasped.

The man's razor-thin back was chestnut brown, like the rest of his skin, but there were brilliant yellow slashes across his back.

In fact, he looked more like a lizard than a man...

Gray sucked in a breath as he flashed back to the sight of the man's tongue just as he fell into his unnatural sleep...the thin, forked thing that had flicked out from between his teeth and flashed across his lips.

"A *mo'o*," Gray breathed in horror. He hissed over to Polunu: "Hey! He's a *mo'o*!"

"I know," Polunu whispered back. "You couldn't tell when he put you to bed with sleep magic?"

"No...I thought I needed more coffee," he hissed. "I didn't know sleep magic was a thing."

"You know it now." Polunu exhaled slowly and shook his head. "*Mo'o*," he said, his entire body trembling. "This is bad."

"Oh, 'cause it was so good before?"

The *mo'o* stretched out his shirt and tied the sleeves to two different bamboo stalks on either side of the fire, constructing a poor but serviceable umbrella over the flames. He added even more logs to the fire, and when the blaze was almost as tall as the old man himself and the flames licked at the makeshift tarp, the *mo'o* pulled a folding knife from his pocket and flicked it open. He stalked back toward his prisoners, testing the blade with his thumb. He crossed between Gray and Polunu and looked back and forth between them.

"What's he doing?" Gray hissed, his eyes wide and fixed on the *mo'o*.

"I think he's deciding who to eat first," Polunu replied.

The lizard creature looked down at the mainlander, his tongue flicking out from between his lips. Gray gulped. The *mo'o* smiled.

His decision was made.

"Hey! *Kupua*! Why don't you start with a *real* man?" Polunu asked, struggling against his ropes. Gray tried not to take the insult personally. "What's the matter? You pick the small one 'cause you afraid of the big one? I always heard stories about how fierce the *mo'o* is. I guess they meant some *other* lizard demon, huh?"

The creature narrowed his eyes. He flicked his tongue at Polunu. "Makes no difference to me," he hissed. He turned and walked toward Polunu. "I was afraid I would fill up on your fat...but I can always have leftovers."

Gray stared, bewildered, as the *mo'o* approached Polunu, the knife held low against his waist. Gray prayed that the big oaf had something planned and wasn't just being noble. If he was going to watch anyone be gutted, he would rather it be himself instead of his friend.

Polunu stopped struggling with his ropes. He sat quietly, limply against his bamboo stalk. His weary eyes grew heavy, and his shoulders sloped down toward the earth. The fight was draining out of him. He couldn't break the ropes, and now he would be slaughtered like a fat lamb and devoured by the lizard-thing.

Gray closed his eyes. He couldn't watch. Then he peeled one eye open, because he *had* to watch. He had to bear witness.

He owed Polunu that much, at least.

The *mo'o* stood over the bound man, his narrow chest expanding and contracting with excited breath. He squatted in front of Polunu, and the big Hawai'ian turned his head to the side. But the *mo'o* grabbed Polunu's chin and forced him to look into his demon face. "Mortals shouldn't meddle with the plans of the gods," the old man hissed. He snapped his jaws, and Polunu flinched. "I'll save a piece for Kamapua'a so he can taste how afraid you were in the end. But the rest..." He leaned in close and ran his lizard tongue up Polunu's cheek, tasting the sweat and tears that were drying on his skin. "The rest, I think I will greatly enjoy." He drew back the knife and rammed it toward Polunu's belly.

Everything that followed happened in a flash. The big Hawai'ian moved like a snake. The ropes fell from his wrists, and Polunu swung his belly to the side, just barely avoiding the knife slash. He swung his right hand hard and brought his fist crunching down against the left side of the old man's face. The *mo'o* collapsed to the ground, mud spattering across the yellow slashes on his bare back. Polunu dove forward, tackling the demon and hammering into him with his huge fists, but the *mo'o* was powerful, and he pushed himself to his feet, lifting Polunu right along with him. The *mo'o* tossed him down like a sack of flour, and Gray could hear the wind explode out of his lungs in a rush. Polunu groaned for air as the lizard brought his foot down on Polunu's leg, hard. He screamed in pain and clutched his thigh to his belly, rolling in agony. The *mo'o* looked around for the knife and saw it lying on the ground a few yards away. He skittered over to pick it up, but when he did, Polunu reached down beneath his leg and grabbed up a fistful of the heart-shaped plants that grew along the forest floor. The *mo'o* returned with the knife in hand and straddled the fallen Hawai'ian. "Weak like all mortals," the creature sniped, sounding almost regretful.

"Strong enough to take a lizard," Polunu grunted. He shoved the fistful of leaves into the demon's mouth. The *mo'o* shot backward, startled. He dropped the knife and clawed at the plants, digging them out of his throat. Polunu swept up another handful of leaves and jumped to his feet, favoring his injured leg, and he crammed those down the lizard's mouth, too. The *mo'o* let loose a guttural groan and tried to spit out the leaves, but Polunu swung up hard and fast with his right fist and connected a bone-shattering uppercut to the lizard's jaw. Teeth cracked as they broke free and rattled around his skull. Polunu clasped one hand around the back of the old man's head and pressed the second against his mouth so he couldn't open it. The *mo'o* pried at Polunu's fingers, and he started to peel them away, but just then, his eyes rolled back up into his head, and he began to sway on his feet. His hands dropped dreamily to his sides. His head bobbed. Polunu let go and took a few steps back. The *mo'o* staggered to his left...then he corrected and plunged to his right. He crashed into a bamboo plant and twirled around it, spinning off into another bunch of stalks. Then he stumbled across the forest like a punch-drunk boxer. His limbs hung limp as noodles; his knees shook, and his head tilted and swayed in every direction. He wobbled back toward the fire, his shoulders bumping against the swaying stalks...and suddenly, he lost his footing. He reached out for a bamboo stalk to steady himself, but he missed, and the *mo'o* went pitching forward, diving headlong into his own flames. The logs cracked and hissed from the weight, but the lizard-thing did not cry out, even though his flesh began to sizzle and roast. His head lolled around on his shoulders, and a smile crept up his reptilian lips. Then the bulk of the *mo'o* melted away like sea foam, streams of it trickling down the burning logs, until there was nothing left but a gaunt, blackened lizard falling down into the embers of the fire.

"I feel like I keep saying this," Gray said, his eyes wide with astonishment. "But what the *hell* was *that*?"

Polunu put his hands on his hips and worked to catch his breath. "That," he gasped, "was *'awa* plant." He picked up the *mo'o*'s knife and lumbered over to Gray. He sliced through the rope, and Gray pulled his hands free.

"Is 'awa Hawai'ian for 'fiery suicide death wish'?" he asked, rubbing his wrists.

"Well, it sort of relaxes you," Polunu said. "It's not like a drug or nothing, but, you know. It makes you feel calm. You can make a drink with it and everything."

"It makes you calm enough to throw yourself onto a fire?" Gray wrinkled his nose at the smoldering logs and tried to peek down into the embers without getting too close.

"*Mo'o* are supposed to be very sensitive to it. Makes them go all loopy. I never had a chance to try it before, though. Never got attacked by a *mo'o* in a wild awa field." He shrugged. "Guess it works."

Gray cleared his throat. "Guess so."

"You okay?" Polunu asked, biting his lower lip and frowning.

"Yeah. Wrists are a little burned up, but that's it. How about you? Did it get you?"

Polunu shook his head. "Nah." He grinned an exhausted grin. "I'm too fast for lizard demons." He glanced over at the fire. "Guess we should go make sure he's dead, yeah?"

"Sure," Gray said. "Guess so."

Neither of them made an attempt to move.

"Or we could just assume it died and get the hell out of here," Gray suggested.

"That sounds better."

Polunu skirted the fire, not turning his back on the hopefully-dead *mo'o*, and picked up Manaiakalani. "I should have known," he said, wiping the mud from the hook and shaking his head sadly. "When the *mo'o* drank the water from his bucket…he said, '*Mahalo*, Lono; *mahalo*, Nāmaka.'"

"What does that mean?"

"Lono is the god of rainfall; Nāmaka is the goddess of ocean. He was thanking them for the water that falls as rain and runs out to the sea."

"If we're singling out every person who talks about the gods like that, I'm pretty sure you're a *moʻo* too, and I'm gonna have to set you on fire."

"It's not that he thanked the gods. It's that he thanked *those* gods. In the upcountry, they like to worship their own gods, remember? I don't think a human this far up the mountain would thank the old gods of Hawai'i for the water, but maybe their own *akua* instead, you know?"

"So just to be clear," Gray said pointedly, "worshipping hill gods, bad; worshipping ancient mythological but comparatively popular gods, good."

Polunu raised an eyebrow. "You ain't still a non-believer, are you, cuz? Not after all this?"

"The gods that keep trying to kill me with witches and lizards and lava aren't giving me much choice *but* to believe," Gray said miserably. Then he sighed. "Still doesn't make it easy to wrap my brain around." They stood there in silence for a few moments, until something snagged in Gray's brain. "Nāmaka. Why do I know that name?"

"Pele's other sister. The one who wants to snuff her out."

"Ah. Right. Fun family they got there."

"Gonna be your in-laws pretty soon," Polunu grinned.

Gray rolled his eyes. Then he pressed the heels of his hands into his sockets, trying to rub some sense into his brain. "This is just insane," he murmured.

"It's strange times here," Polunu agreed. "I told you when you said you wanna find Pele: you goin' down a whole new path. This isn't exactly what I thought, it'd be, you know? But here we are." Both men fell quiet. Polunu pushed his toes into the mud. "You know what I think?" he said.

"That it's time for second lunch?"

Polunu smiled. "Nah. What I think is, *nā akua* were never meant to compete with progress. They lost their battle for the world a long, long time ago...now they got nothin' to do but hide and wait 'til the world destroys itself and they can take back their power. But now, one of them don't wanna wait no more. He wants to destroy the world himself. Get things really moving. Take down everyone in the way. Go back to the way things were. More primal...more brutal." He looked down at Maui's hook and ran his finger along the edge of the ancient bone. "You know?" he added, almost to himself.

"Yeah," Gray sighed. "I know. I really do." He stuffed his hands into his pockets and began heading back down the hill.

"Hey, cuz! You going the wrong way." Polunu jerked his thumb up toward the summit. "The mountain goes up!"

"And I'm going down," Gray said. "Enough is enough. I'm going back to the hotel. You coming with, or should I notify your next of kin?"

He didn't wait for Polunu to answer. He just pushed through the bamboo, retracing his steps down the mountain toward the car.

# Chapter 18

The wild pigs rutted and screamed, spurred on by the sudden rain, but Hi'iaka did not hear them.

She was too far gone inside the storm.

The clouds had answered her call, melting together in a thick gauze of gray that shouldered out the sun. The rain had fallen slowly at first, but now it was picking up steam, pouring down in a torrent of slanting pellets that rattled the earth with their force and sent little creeks streaming down the mountain.

She murmured a quick prayer to Lono, the god of the rain, even though he probably couldn't hear her voice, muffled by the circle as she was. But she whispered it anyway, in genuine thanks, and as a signal that his work was done for today. It was her time now.

Now was the time for thunder. Now was the time for lightning.

She closed her eyes and lifted her arms to the ceiling. She whispered the ancient words, words from no language still spoken on the earth save for those with memories that stretched back to the days of wild ocean and wind. She spoke the words, and she felt their power crackle to life as the breath crossed her lips, but she also felt the stifling pressure of the magic that stuck in the invisible net of Kamapua'a's circle, and she had no way of knowing how many of her words were reaching the sky so high above her little prison. So she reached, and she reached, and she reached with her mind, willing her spell to send its magic into the atmosphere, waiting for the rumble of thunder in her ears.

But the thunder didn't come. The lightning didn't flash. The rain fell harder, and the jungle beyond the shed was lost in the gray veil of water, but the thunder and the lightning held their peace. She pushed herself harder, straining against the confines of the circle, but her power sounded back at her, buzzing in her ears, catching in her throat. It was raucous, it was stifling…and soon it was too much to bear. She gasped as her arms fell to her sides, and the power drained from her lips. Kamapua'a's magic was too strong. His circle was too restrictive. She could not break through it, and her voice was silenced to the heavens.

There would be no thunder rumbling through the clouds. There would be no lightning striking the mud and obliterating her cell. There would be no storm.

There was little hope left.

She closed her eyes and moved her lips. *Find me, Grayson,* they said. *Do not die, and do not be turned away. You are my only hope. Do not give up on me.*

# Chapter 19

"I give up!" Gray cried.

"*Haole!*" Polunu called out after him. "Wait!"

"Will you stop calling me that?" Gray pushed his way angrily through the trees, soaked to the bone. "I get it, I get it. I'm from Missouri. I'm a dumb white idiot. I'm not Hawai'ian. If I *were* Hawai'ian, maybe all this would actually *mean* something, and there'd be a reason to keep going, but I'm just a dumb *haole*, I've got no business here, and man...I just could not agree more."

"You know I don't mean it bad!" Polunu huffed and puffed his way down the slope, struggling to keep up on his injured leg. "Just wait—let's talk about it!"

"There's nothing to talk about," Gray sighed. He stopped and whirled around, jamming his finger toward the top of the mountain. "Up there? That's death. That is pain and torture and misery and *death*. It's enough. All right? *Enough.*"

"But Hi'iaka—"

"I feel terrible about Hi'iaka! You think I don't? I know it's my fault she got caught, and I feel *terrible* about that! Honestly, I don't know how I'm going to live with myself after this. I really, really don't. But at least I can still *live*! If we keep going, all three of us are going to die—you, me, *and* the goddess who, if we're being honest, really should be able to fend for herself up there, *because she's a goddess*! And we don't even know what pig-face wants with her! We're just running headlong into danger, *assuming* that he's going to deal her some horrible, terrible death, but guess what? You don't kidnap people you want to murder; you kidnap people you need to keep alive, so she's sitting up there at the top of this mountain, *alive*, and he might be treating her like a *queen* for all we know! We could be risking our lives to save her from the most comfortable captivity the world has ever known. And if he *is* hurting her? Guess what again? *She's a goddess*, and he's just a demigod, and that means she's *fine!*"

"You *know* she's not fine," Polunu said. "She wouldn't have asked you for help if she didn't need it. We got to do—"

"Nothing! We 'got to do' *nothing*. I have been hit, and bitten, and swarmed by shark-monsters, and buried alive, and smashed by trees, and tied to bamboo, and I've almost been eaten—*twice*: once by an old man who was really a *lizard demon*, and once by a hill witch who *didn't even have a face*, and I have *no* idea how she was going to put my skin in her mouth, but she was *definitely* gonna do it! *And I have lava scars!*" he shouted, pulling down the collar of his shirt and showing the smooth marks where Pele's molten rocks had seared into his skin. "This is it! This is enough! I didn't come to Hawai'i to die."

Polunu stared in disbelief. He shook his head and said, "You came a long way to abandon this altar, *haole*."

Gray's eyes narrowed, and he stepped up to the larger man, poking a finger into his chest. "What did you say?"

Polunu glowered down at the mainlander. "I said, it's a long way to come to abandon people you love at their altar. *Haole*." He spat out the last word. It dripped with disappointment as it spilled from between his lips.

"First of all," Gray seethed, "how *dare* you throw the altar in my face. How *dare* you. And second of all, you name one person on this godforsaken island that I 'love,' and I'll march right up that hill and punch the pig-god right in the face!"

"Me, you dummy!" Polunu said, giving Gray a little shove that sent him pin-wheeling back. "And Hi'iaka! And Pele, and Maui, and all the people who work at your stupid mainlander resort, and all those idiots who almost ran you off the road today, and everyone, but mostly Hi'iaka! And me too, you know?" Polunu wiped his nose on his wrist, then crossed his arms and stood firm.

"Are you serious? I don't love you, or Hi'iaka, or any of the *janitors* at the *hotel*!" Gray cried. "I love *me*, and I want to save me by going back to the hotel, packing my bags, and getting the hell out of Maui, *stat*!"

"You so stupid," Polunu muttered, shaking his head, "you don't even know that we are *'ohana*."

Gray threw his hands up in frustration. "What the hell is *'ohana*?" he demanded.

"It's *family*, stupid! You and me, we are brothers! We are *'ohana*. We are in this *together*, 'cause we got a *bond*, you know? And Hi'iaka, she is your *'ohana* too. She cares for you, brah. You think she would risk getting attacked by a demigod like Kamapua'a for someone she don't care about? Are you serious? She cares about you, and you care about her, too, otherwise what are we doing in the upcountry? It's scary as hell up here! But we came because she's *'ohana* too now. She's your family, and *I'm* your family, and everyone else on this island, they are *all* your *family*, *haole*. And on O'ahu, too, and Kaua'i, and the Big Island, and Moloka'i, and Lāna'i, and Ni'ihau, all those people, they your *'ohana*." He laced his fingers together and held them out over his belly. "We are all *connected.* I know you feel that. And if you don't, then you go back to the car, you drive back to the hotel, you go home to St. Louis and never think about old Polunu again. But if you feel it here," he said, reaching out and touching Gray lightly on the chest, "then you better come with me up that mountain and face whatever scary shit Kamapua'a can throw, with me—*together*—and we will do everything we can to save that girl who touched your heart." Polunu paused a second to let his words take hold. "Now what you gonna do, *haole*? You gonna go home? Or you gonna go up that mountain and maybe get eaten alive by lizards and pigs, and fight for your '*ohana*?"

Gray gritted his teeth. He looked up the mountain. There was no telling what sorts of horrors still stood between them and Kamapua'a. The closer they got to the demigod, the more difficult the traps were bound to become. They'd survived so far, but only just barely, and if they pushed on up the mountain, they would almost certainly die. And he had a hunch it wouldn't be painless, or quick.

But Hi'iaka *was* on her own sort of altar up there—a sacrificial altar. Even though she was a goddess, and even though she may have been strong, and even though Kamapua'a needed her alive, she was in trouble. Gray could feel it in his bones. Could he really leave her there to suffer at the hands of the pig-god? Could he abandon Polunu, leave him with his heart in the wind, go back to the mainland, and never think about Hawai'i or its archaic gods and their pathetic rivalries ever again?

He could, he realized. He really could leave it all behind on the island. He could walk away.

He really, really could.

But he didn't want to.

He wanted to stay and fight for his ʻohana.

"Do you seriously think we can handle this?" Gray asked.

Polunu nodded once, and no more. "Yes, I do. Or else I'd still be at my pineapple stand, and you'd be up here alone."

Gray took a deep breath. He closed his eyes. "All right," he decided. "Let's keep going. Let's go rescue a goddess or get roasted by lizard demons trying." He marched past Polunu and stalked back through the trees.

Polunu smiled.

Then he turned and followed his brother up the hill.

# Chapter 20

Gray just wanted to die.

He shook his head firmly and scrubbed his hands down his face. "There is no way the pigs went this way," he said, his voice muffled by his palms.

"The tracks don't lie, cuz. They crossed that bridge, all right."

Gray peeked out between his fingers. The old rope bridge had to be 8,000 years old, at least. Half the wooden slats were broken or missing, while the other half were slick with moss and rain, and the ropes that strung them from one side of the gulch to the other were sun-faded and frayed to the point of being glorified twine. It spanned a canyon of 150 feet or so, almost as wide as a football field. The drop, though...that was closer to 500 feet—on the conservative side—and it ended in a pounding rush beneath the waterfall they'd glimpsed from further down the mountain. The falls rose high to their left, and they fell so far and so hard that Gray had to scream to be heard over the sound when he said, "No way!"

"Come on—what're you afraid of? If a herd of pigs can do it, you can do it."

"I'm not sure all the pigs made it over," Gray said, eyeing the gaps in the bridge. He grabbed onto a tree that grew near the edge of the cliff for support and peered down at the frothing river below.

The rain was finally letting up, but there must have been a downpour higher up the mountain; the waterfall was surging, and the river was angry. "That is almost definitely a pig down there," he said, pointing down at something that was pretty clearly a rock.

"Hey, we can turn around if you're gonna be scared of heights like a man-baby," Polunu shrugged.

Gray grunted. "No way. I get enough family guilt from my *actual* family in Missouri. I think I've had enough from you for one lifetime, too." He reached out carefully and put his hand on one of the ropes. He could feel the vibration from the wind. The bottoms of his feet began to tingle. "Hey, how about this? You go first."

"Look at me, cuz." Polunu spread his arms out wide, inviting a good glance. "I weigh, like, three hundred pounds more than you. If it breaks for anyone, it's me."

"That's how we'll test whether it's safe for me!"

"But if I break the bridge, no one can get through. If you go first, then even if I snap the ropes, you're still good to go! Trust me, braddah, you'll be good. That bridge'll hold you for *sure*."

"Great. Really comforting." He shook the rope, and even though the bridge swayed, it *did* seem pretty solid. He eased one foot onto the first plank and tested it with a little weight. It groaned a little, but it held. "What happens if I get attacked by a *moʻo* halfway over?"

"Maybe we're done with *nā moʻo*," Polunu said with a hopeful shrug. "Maybe we don't see no more of them, you know?"

"I teach stories for a living," Gray sighed. "If I know one thing for sure, it's that mythological monsters will always come in threes." Then he stepped onto the rope bridge and out over the chasm before his brain could talk the rest of his body out of it.

*Don't look down*, he reminded himself, slowly and carefully stepping one foot in front of the other. The planks were surprisingly wide, and they actually felt almost sturdy beneath his shoe. He grabbed the ropes on either side so hard that his palms ached, but that was a small price to pay for not tumbling through a crack. *Don't look down. Just don't look down.*

Gray had seen a lot of movies. He knew that when people told themselves not to look down, that was *exactly* when they always looked down. So he was stern with himself. He meant it when he said to keep his eyes up.

But then his left foot came down on nothing but empty air, and he fell into the hole where a board used to be.

He shrieked as his leg dropped clean through the bridge, and he fell forward, his left leg dangling above the river, his right foot slipping on the wet boards. He grabbed the ropes even harder, pulling on them for support...and they didn't like that. The rope on the right tilted down, taking the bridge with it, swinging him into a forty five-degree angle to the cliff. He hooked his left leg over the edge of the last sturdy board, but he slid down into the loose netting of ropes that zigzagged along the side of the bridge, which made the bridge twist even more, and now when he looked down at his feet, he saw the top of the falls. His head hung out sideways over open air.

He screamed and screamed.

Polunu rushed forward onto the first few planks and threw his weight to the left side of the bridge. The ropes rocked back a little, enough for Gray, even twenty feet away, to lunge upward, grab the ropes on the other side, and pull himself flat against the board to give the bridge some balance. He lay there, shaking and wailing, with his mouth flat against the wet, wooden plank, one arm clutching the ropes, the other wrapped around the board. His feet were hooked around the ropes on the other side, and he was determined to just lie there until the whole bridge collapsed and he fell to his death.

"I don't want to do this anymore!" he yelled, squeezing his eyes shut.

"You doing great!" Polunu shouted back, trying to sound encouraging and failing completely. "Almost there! Just...be careful. You know?"

"I don't want to die!" Gray wailed.

"If pigs can do it, you can do it!"

"Pigs get eaten all the time!"

Polunu furrowed his brow. "So what?"

"I don't know, it just isn't very comforting right now to know that they're not smart enough to not get eaten!"

"You can do it, braddah! You're almost there!"

Gray lifted his head and chanced a look at how much further he had to go. "I am not," he called back.

"You want me to come carry you?"

"No!"

"I'll do it. Honest. I don't mind. I'll come pick you up and carry you. Hold on, I'm coming." The big man took a step back onto the bridge.

"No, no, no!" Gray shrieked. He shot out a hand to keep Polunu at bay. "No more weight! Just...I'll be fine. I'll do it. I'm gonna do it." He paused for a few seconds. "Am I doing it?"

"No," Polunu frowned.

Gray cursed. He was telling his body to get up, but it was refusing to listen. "Stupid body," he whispered. "Cross the bridge, and I'll give you donuts." His legs responded to that, pushing him shakily up to his feet, and his hands resumed their death grips on the ropes on either side. He tried to block out the crush of the waterfall, which seemed to be growing louder and angrier every second. He lifted his foot and stepped gingerly over the space of the missing slat, setting down lightly on the next plank and testing it for strength.

It held.

Then he moved slowly forward, testing each board before giving it his full weight, rubbing his hands raw on the ropes. Each sway of the bridge caused his heart to plunge into his feet. At one point, he slipped on a wet plank, and his foot almost shot through the ropes. But his shoe got tangled in the webbing, and he stayed upright on the bridge, so he pushed on, with the river surging and frothing so far below.

Soon he was crossing the halfway point, where the bridge began to slope upward toward the other side. This made the crossing a little easier, since keeping his eyes on the planks no longer meant looking straight down into the misty chasm, and he quickened his pace. The bridge wobbled harder in response, and Gray threw himself up toward the far ledge, his belly hitting half on the bridge, half on solid ground. He'd never felt so good being so uncomfortable in his entire life.

"I made it!" he called out. "I made it!"

"How did it feel?" Polunu called back from the other side of the canyon. "Strong?"

"You know, it did. It *did* make me feel pretty strong," Gray affirmed proudly, climbing to his feet and wicking the slimy water from his shirt.

"Not you, dummy. The bridge. Did the bridge feel strong?"

"Oh." Gray tinged pink with embarrassment. "No. The bridge did not feel strong at all."

"Great," Polunu said miserably. "Say a prayer for me, cuz. I'm coming over."

Gray held his breath as Polunu shifted his entire bulk onto the slats of the bridge. The ropes groaned, and the whole bridge swayed ominously, but the pieces held.

"Okay," he said, his breath shallow, "here I come."

Polunu moved with an ease and grace befitting a much leaner man. When the bridge shifted one way, he gently countered; when it shifted back, he leaned into the sway. He held the ropes gently, especially in his right hand, which was also tasked with carrying Manaiakalani. He stepped carefully and cleanly over the missing planks, his feet never seeming to slip despite being clad only in his smooth, worn flip-flops.

"What are you, a mountain goat?" Gray asked, wholly unable to hide his jealousy at the big man's fluid movements.

"I am Hawai'ian," Polunu called back, concentrating on the climb up the second half of slippery boards, "just like the bridge. We have an understanding."

"It must be xenophobic," Gray grumbled.

Polunu pulled his way up the gently sloping bridge and carefully stepped onto firm ground next to Gray. The ropes sighed with relief. "See?" he grinned. "Nothing to it. You just—" But his words died out in his throat.

Gray wrinkled his brow as Polunu's eyes grew wide. "What? What is it? What's—?"

Polunu lifted a trembling finger, pointing over Gray's shoulder. "*Mo'o*," he said with great terror, his voice all but swallowed up by the roar of the falls. Then he hissed, "Gray—run!"

Gray turned slowly, his heart pounding, and he heard the demon before he saw it—heard its wet, ragged breath and a deep, guttural growl that Gray felt rumbling through his skin and rattling his bones in their joints. He *smelled* it, too, a heavy mixture of sulfur and mud. And when he finished his revolution, his mouth hung open, and a quiet wheeze of horror escaped from his lungs, because what stood before him—what *towered over* him—wasn't a lizard or an old man with skin stretched tight over his ribs.

It was a dragon.

The beast stood three stories tall, with dark green scales and blue and yellow spots spattered across its back and head, and two long, spiked horns thrusting viciously out from its brow. Flames burned in its nostrils, and when it opened its massive jaw, it let slip the shade of a bright fiery light glowing in the recesses of its throat. The monster's cry was an unearthly shriek that pierced the air with such force that the waters spilling down the falls shifted, bowing out like ribbon against the rush of wind. The dragon reared back onto its powerful back legs and spread its arms wide, stretching its mammoth bat wings through the treetops. The creature's exposed belly was light green, a perfect match for its huge, pale, serpent eyes.

The dragon screamed again, and a stream of fire spewed from its throat, filling up the sky and setting fire to the leaves of a swath of trees. They crackled and flared like they'd been doused in napalm, continuing to burn long after the dragon reined in its fire.

Gray couldn't speak. He couldn't move.

"Gray!" Polunu hissed again, giving him a shove. "*Run!*"

The dragon fell back down onto all fours, rocking the earth and slamming both men to the ground. It opened its mouth, and Gray saw the flames begin to roil in the back of its throat.

Suddenly, his legs found their motivation to work.

He stumbled forward, darting into the cover of the trees. He heard Polunu lumber off somewhere in the opposite direction, splitting the dragon's focus. Gray dove into a copse of purple-flowered jacarandas, pressing himself up against twisting trunk of one of the trees. He felt the air sizzle with heat, and suddenly, his entire field of vision was billowing clouds of orange and red. He could feel the moisture evaporating from his skin as the dragon's fire rolled past him on either side, split in two by the trunk of the tree. He flattened himself up even more, and screamed. Then the fire pushed on, evaporating into hazy streams of hot air and drifting up through the branches.

Gray gasped. He did a frantic inventory of his body parts, and all were accounted for. His sleeves were smoldering, and his arms glowed pink with some degree of burn, but he was alive. "Thank you, tree," he whispered, pushing himself up from the ground. He turned and saw the exposed half of the trunk, and most of the branches, engulfed in flames. The dragon leaned down close to the ground, snaking its neck between the trees, slipping its head down to within a few feet of Gray's own. "Polunu!" he cried, searching for an escape. "Help!"

The *mo'o* sneered. It opened its jaws. It lunged forward to snap down on its meal. But the gleaming black teeth fell short. Instead of slicing through Gray's torso, they reared back as the monster screeched in pain. Gray took the chance to dive out of the way, into a thicket of gardenias. He peered out from behind the leaves and saw Polunu hugging onto the dragon's tail, the Hook of Maui buried deep in the monster's flesh.

The dragon screamed again, and its mouth exploded with a blazing stream of fire, but it couldn't hit Polunu without searing its own tail. It roared in frustration and slammed its tail hard on the ground, but Polunu held on for his life, digging his big fingers up under the dragon's scales and wrapping his legs around the tapered end of the tail. The *moʻo* flapped its wings and rose into the air, but didn't appear to be much of a flier. It hovered only a few feet off the ground. Instead of flying, it flung its tail against a tree, smashing straight through the vertical roots. The whole tree buckled, and Polunu ducked just in time to avoid decapitation by banyan.

The dragon wheeled around, crashing its tail into tree after tree. Each time, Polunu ducked or adjusted in time to avoid being splattered across the mountain, but he couldn't keep it up for much longer. His face was red and streaming with sweat, and even at this distance, with the flurry of motion, Gray could see that his arms were shaking from the strain of holding on. He wondered why Polunu didn't just let go and try to roll to safety...but then he saw the Hawai'ian reach up, trying to grasp the exposed handle of Manaiakalani, and he understood.

Maui's words echoed in his ears. *Pele wants you to hook Kamapuaʻa in the chest, and then Pele wants you to yank the hook out, because Pele knows that when you do, you'll draw out the divine soul of him, leaving him mortal and vulnerable.*

It wasn't enough to drive the point of Manaiakalani into a divine creature. That was just a flesh wound. The magic came in pulling the hook back out and taking the divinity with it.

Polunu had lost his grip when he stabbed the tail. Now he was fighting to get it back.

The dragon whirled, spewing fire into the air. It lumbered back toward the canyon, stumbling through the trees, blinded by its anger. Its tail thrashed from side to side. Polunu reached out and touched the handle of Manaiakalani with the tips of his fingers. Then the dragon whipped around, hard, and Polunu lost his grip on the tail. He was launched through the air, sailing out over the open ravine.

"Polunu!" Gray screamed. He burst out from his hiding spot and ran to the edge of the cliff as Polunu arced over the canyon. His heart froze in his chest as Polunu fell...and somehow—miraculously, incredibly, *unbelievably*—crashed onto the rope bridge, hitting it right in the center. The bridge buckled, and the ropes along the northern side snapped. The slats gave away, and the whole bridge tilted onto its side, now held above the furious river by only one set of ropes. Polunu lunged out with an exhausted arm and caught one of the supports. He hoisted himself up and grabbed onto the edge of a vertical plank, feeding his arm through the gap between the slats and holding himself up against the collapsing bridge.

But Gray didn't know how long he could possibly hold on.

He knew it couldn't be long, though.

Gray turned toward the *mo'o* and told his terrified brain to shut up and stop screaming.

He had to destroy the dragon.

The *mo'o* snapped its tail from side to side, working to dislodge the hook, but it was mostly focused on Polunu. It fanned out its wings and roared a stream of fire out across the falling bridge. The ball of flame evaporated into smoke before it reached Polunu, and the ropes and the wood were so soaked through with rain that the fire only caught in a few places, burning low and hissing in the falling drizzle. The dragon stomped its huge feet in frustration, shaking the world. Gray bounced low on his knees and managed to stay on his feet. The dragon reared back to let a second fireball fly, and Gray took his chance. He sprinted forward and dove for the monster's tail. As the *mo'o* snarled its fiery breath at the bridge, Gray slammed into the plate-like scales of the tail. The impact knocked the breath from his lungs. Gasping for air, he clawed his arm up toward the hook. He threw himself forward in a desperate gamble, and his fingers seized on Manaiakalani. The dragon flicked its tail, and Gray slipped. He went flying back into the jungle. He hit the ground hard and rolled to a stop against an outcropping of rock. Dazed, he looked down at his hand.

He held Maui's hook.

He had ripped it out of the dragon's flesh.

The *mo'o* let its stream of fire roar out over the bridge, and the force of its anger pushed the rolling flames farther. The fireballs streamed up against Polunu, and he cried out in pain. But he was at the very edge of the heat, and when the fire dissipated, his shirt was smoking, his skin was beet red, but he was still whole, and he still clung to the hanging bridge.

The dragon whirled around and shrieked angrily at its tail. A chunk of its dark green flesh had been ripped out with Manaiaka-lani, and a stream of thick, azure liquid spouted out the hole like a geyser. The *mo'o* screamed again, but the fire had died in its nostrils and throat; steam poured out instead. The monster thrashed its arms, slicing the air with its talons, screeching in pain...but the creature's divinity continued to spill out, and the *mo'o* began to shrink like a withering vine.

Gray screwed up his face and stuck out his tongue in revulsion. "Divinity is...blue?" He stared in grotesque wonder, then ducked as the dragon's tail whipped past his head, narrowly avoiding having his skull caved in. A stream of the blue liquid spattered across his shoulders. His stomach lurched; the divinity juice smelled like moss and flour and pepper and bile. He swallowed down the urge to wretch and watched the dragon shrivel into nothing.

*Relatively* nothing.

The *moʻo* shrank and shrank, twisting and contorting; its horns melted down into its skull, and its wings pinched and pulled and finally disintegrated into the air, until it was no longer a dragon, no longer a *moʻo* at all. Drained of its divinity and magic, the lizard-demon was now just a small, unremarkable, blue-and-yellow-mottled skink lizard.

Gray looked down at the tiny thing, amazed. The lizard blinked back up at him. It flicked out its tongue and cocked its head…then it scurried off into the trees and disappeared from sight.

"Gray! Help!"

Gray gasped himself out of his thoughts and looked toward the bridge. The dragon's first blast of fire hadn't done much to burn the ropes, but it had gone a long way toward drying them…and its second stream of fire now crackled across the bridge, the flames feeding on the hissing, popping fibers of rope. There were three cords woven together to form the handrail that was now the only support for the entire bridge.

One of them snapped as Gray looked on.

"Polunu!" he screamed. He sprinted down to the cliff's edge but stood helplessly at the rope's anchor. Polunu was halfway across the bridge, and Gray couldn't think. "What do I do?!"

"I don't know! I don't know!" Polunu's cries were battered by the roar of the falls. Tears streaked his cheeks; he was losing his grip on the wet planks.

"Hold on! Hold on!" Gray screamed. He pushed his hands through his hair, he paced along the cliff, and he didn't know what to do. He couldn't reach Polunu. He couldn't hold the bridge. The fire continued to burn, and the second rope snapped. The entire bridge dropped a few feet, and Polunu screamed. "*Hold on!*" Gray yelled against the falls. He had to put out the fire. It was out of reach, way too far out of reach, but he had to try.

It was the only thing he could do.

"I'm gonna put out the fire!" He looked around wildly, spinning a full circle, looking for something, *anything* that might be able to extinguish the flames. All he saw were trees and plants and rocks. He cursed. The bridge groaned.

"Grayson!" Polunu screamed desperately. "Help!"

"*I don't know what to do!*" he screamed back. Tears spilled from his eyes. He dropped to his knees, threw Manaiakalani to the side, and began clawing at the wet earth. He tossed fistfuls of red soil at the flames. Most of it spread in the air and sailed out above the river, but even the dirt that hit the fire had no effect.

There just wasn't enough of it.

"*I can smother it!*" Gray screamed, tearing through the ground. His nails struck stone; they chipped and bled, but still he dug, pulling up dirt and heaving it at the flames. He dug and he threw, and he dug and he threw, and he dug and he threw, but he couldn't dig enough or throw enough, and the bridge burned higher and hotter.

The flames crackled. The bridge roasted.

And then, the third rope snapped.

Polunu hung suspended in the air for only a moment...then the ropes dropped away, the planks lurched, Polunu lost his grip, and he fell, helpless and dazed, though the mist and the air. He spun through the wind, reaching out with his hand, grasping for help that would not come. Gray watched in silent, open-mouthed horror as Polunu drifted away, falling in slow motion; entire nations were built and destroyed in the time that he fell. Then his friend, his brother—his ʻ*ohana*—dropped into the raging river as silently as a stone. He was swallowed by the water and mist, and he was gone, swept away by the current, pulled down the mountain, and washed out into the sea.

# Chapter 21

Grayson lay on his back in the disheveled earth and waited for his tears to run dry. But he had tapped into a well that was as deep as the ocean, and he cried until so much salt had flowed that it began to burn in the tracks of the tears across his temples.

And then he cried some more.

His brain felt numb, soaked through in the anesthetic of his shock. His thoughts were wrapped in blankets, and there were thousands of them, twirling sluggishly through his gray matter, bumping softly against the edges of his mind, but not unwrapping themselves, so he could only guess at the shapes of their softness.

The waterfall roared, the wind blew, the fires died, time ticked on, and Gray lay on his back in the disheveled earth and waited for the world to stop.

He should call someone. But he didn't know who. He pulled himself up to a seat and fumbled through his pocket for his phone. It took him almost a full minute to remember that an emergency line existed for tragedies like this, and that its number was 9-1-1. He tapped the screen to life and dialed…but he was in the upcountry, well beyond the limits of his civilized comforts, and there was no signal.

He couldn't even make the phone call.

He couldn't even do that.

The screen went dark in his hands, and he stared down at the phone. It looked so foreign here, in this place, in this time. It didn't fit in his new world of magic, gods, and monsters.

Grayson had been a fool. He'd been chasing myths since that night on the hotel deck, accepting them as some fluke of existence that would reset itself when he left Hawai'i. He'd gone on this mad journey, pushing the unbelievable but unavoidable truth to the side, ignoring it as much as he could, scattering the pieces of it to the hidden corners of his brain, never giving them enough time or attention to allow themselves to reassemble into a complete and solid thought. He had charged ahead in a state of self-inflicted blindness, through Pele's cave and the lava wound, past the meeting with Maui and retrieval of Manaiakalani, beyond the witch with no face and the demonic lizards, and none of those things, as extraordinary and mind-blowing as they were, *none* of them could make his brain actually register what was happening. He was too good at compartmentalizing the legends and locking them in drawers and hiding them away to gather the dust of neglect. He hadn't known the incredible strength of his own denial, but there it was. The proof was in the shadows.

But Polunu's fall could not be scattered into the dark. His death couldn't be hidden behind a curtain or swept beneath a rug. It was *real*. It wasn't part of a story to be catalogued in an index. It was the truth. Polunu had fallen to his death, he was gone, and because that was real, that meant the *mo'o* were real. The faceless *mujina* was real. *Nā akua* were real. This was *happening*, this was the *truth* of it, this was the way the world worked now, at least here, at least for this while, and he had no choice now but to accept it and face it like the light of the sun.

He'd pushed the reality from his mind because on some level, he thought it would drive him to the point of insanity. But as he sat at the edge of the cliff, gathering the pieces of thought that he'd scattered to the sides and molding them together into the terrifying truth of *nā akua* and their dangerous games, Grayson's brain didn't break. It didn't scream and tear itself to pieces. It became hard, and resolved. Polunu's death was the crucible in which Gray's understanding was forged. He stuffed his phone into his pocket and rose to his feet, jaw clenched, his fists balled tightly at his sides. Kamapua'a was near, and he had dark plans for Hi'iaka. Beyond his concerns and his feelings for the goddess, and beyond the sense of responsibility for getting her caught, and beyond his maddening need to risk the impossible—looming above all that was the fact that the schemes of gods meant a holocaust for humans. The schemes of gods *always* meant ruin for mankind. The stories were always clear.

Perhaps Polunu had understood that from the beginning.

He had certainly died for it.

And Gray might die, too. That threat was *real*. It was part of the new truth. In all probability, he'd end the day either dead or severely wounded and praying for death. He didn't want to die. And he didn't want to feel pain.

But that's not how the world worked anymore.

He wiped the tears from his face with the back of his wrist. He picked up Manaiakalani and squeezed it tightly in his right hand. He stood at the edge of the cliff. "I'm sorry," he whispered into the chasm. "Polunu...I am so, so sorry." Then he choked the lump in his throat, turned his back on the river, and pushed his way through the brush, picking up the trail of pigs and following it up the mountain.

It was time to end things, one way or another.

# Chapter 22

Kamapua'a leered down at Hi'iaka, his eyes gleaming in the dimness of the shed. "Your army was just cut in half by my *mo'o*. Only one lone soldier draws near. And my trees tell me he is a scrawny *haole*." The pig-god leaned forward, his hands on his knees, bringing his snout near enough to Hi'iaka's face that she could smell the putrid stench of his breath. His tusks dripped with saliva as he whispered, "What do you think he will taste like?"

"You'll never know," Hi'iaka said sharply. But though her voice was strong, her heart was weak. Grayson had proven resilient, surviving a *mujina* and three *mo'o*, yes. But he could not defeat Kamapua'a. The pig-god was too strong, too ruthless, too hungry for whatever power he thought he could drain from Hi'iaka. And with his army of boars to protect him, he was practically invincible. Pele had been a fool to send two mortals alone. Or perhaps she was sending Hi'iaka a message. They had a special bond, that was true, but it wouldn't be the first time one sister had wounded the other.

Though it might prove to be the last.

The pig-god sneered. "Do you know the hour grows late?"

"As the daylight dies, so does your chance to set me free without Pele slaughtering you like the pig you are."

Kampapua'a's eyes blazed, and then he squealed with laughter. "You *are* fiery, Little Egg. Just like your sister." The demigod straightened up to his full height. "I'm not even sure your hero will make it to us before sunset. And soon after that, the full moon will rise. Then I will have your *mana*, and Pele's power will no longer rival mine. It will not come close. Perhaps I will drain *her* at the next full moon…she certainly has that coming." He scratched his whiskered chin as he paced the floor. Mucus dribbled out from his snout and strung across the dirt like a spider's web. "I will be stronger than Kāne and Nāmaka and Papa together. I will be the greatest force in all of Polynesia, Little Egg. I will be a *full* god, a real *akua*, the strongest god the world has ever seen, and the people of Hawai'i will fall to their knees in worship of me. They will scrape and bleed at my whim." He stopped pacing and gave a mean little smile. "Won't that be fun?"

Hi'iaka rolled her eyes. She couldn't stand these pathetic speeches. One of the few good things about the people losing their faith in *nā akua* and moving away to new religions was that there was now seldom cause for grand and grating monologues from her family. "The only flaw in your plan is the glaring fact that you cannot steal my *mana* by stepping into my shadow, pig-god. Have you been so long forgotten that you yourself forget the rules? Shadow-stealing was the magic of the ancients, and it has only ever applied to mortals."

"You are correct, as so rarely happens. It has never worked *before*. But it will work today."

Hi'iaka snorted her laughter and derision. "And how do you expect to make that little *mo'olelo* come true?"

Kamapua'a did not respond, not outright. Instead, he squealed out an order to his boar army in his animal tongue. The pigs answered the call, storming into the shed on hooves of thunder. They rushed toward Hi'iaka, and she braced herself. But they parted like a river around her circle and stampeded at the walls of the shed instead. One-third of the herd ran straight to the back wall; one-third veered to the left, and one-third charged to the right. They plowed into the flimsy tin supports, and the three wavering walls collapsed out onto the forest floor. The roof groaned and fell in, and Hi'iaka raised her arms against it, but Kamapua'a caught the broad sheet of tin in his upturned hands and held it above them like a great platter. He hurled the roof to the side, and it crashed into the trees.

They were out in the open now, and Hi'iaka smiled in spite of her circumstances. It was good to feel the rush of air, to hear the rustle of the leaves, and to see the sky again.

Confinement did not suit her.

The forest smelled of gardenia and mango, and it was reassuring, somehow, to recognize beauty amid such ugliness. The water she had heard through the walls was close; a little river ran past the clearing, just on the other side of the trees where the tin roof now lay. The water cut a path straight down the mountain, gathering speed as it disappeared through a crater of its own design.

*Such beauty in the world*, she thought. *And such ugliness.*

Hi'iaka looked down at her shadow, which stretched long in the light cast by the falling sun. It slashed across Kamapua'a's legs, and she sneered. "You stand in my shadow, Lord of Pigs, as is fitting. And do you feel my *mana* coursing through your veins? Or are you a pathetic fool with a reckoning swinging over his head like an axe?"

Kamapua'a returned the leering smile and crossed his arms. "The sun is for mortals," he said. "The moonlight is for us gods. When you cast your night shadow, *then* will I have your *mana*, Little Egg."

"The moonlight?" Hi'iaka laughed. "Even with the brain of a pig, you should know that a moon will not throw enough light, full or not. The night shadow is a myth."

"So are you," he grinned. "And yet, here you stand."

"I have seen many, many nights, pig-god, and many full moons, and so have you. We both know the moon does not cast shadows."

Kamapua'a's lips curled back over his tusks; his beady eyes burned with fire, and he squealed a terrible screech of glee. "But tonight, I have this." He signaled to his herd, and the boars began rooting through the dirt at the edge of the clearing. They threw soil and leaves with their snouts and hooves, burrowing into the earth. When they'd dug out a long, shallow trough, one boar, a large female, lowered her head into the hole and locked her jaws around something buried within. She pulled out a long wooden staff with a warped shield of glass fastened to one end with a rope of woven palm leaves. The boar carried the staff gingerly in her jaws and laid it at Kamapua'a's feet. Then the boar lowered its head and backed away to rejoin its herd.

The pig-god snorted as he picked up the staff, brushed off the dirt, and held it up for Hi'iaka to see. The glass disk fixed to the top of the pole was the size of a dinner platter, roughly shaped but clear as a windowpane. "Your smithing skills need practice," Hi'iaka said, her chin held high.

"Perhaps. But it's not the craftsmanship of the glass that makes it a thing of beauty."

"Clearly," Hi'iaka said, narrowing her eyes.

Kamapua'a bared his teeth, annoyed, but he continued. "It is the magic that was woven through its substance in the forge. Our friend Kanaloa imbued this little plate of glass with an extraordinary bit of sorcery. You see, it's a lens." He circled behind Hi'iaka and plunged the staff into the ground. It rocked gently on its anchor when the pig-god removed his hand, and the pane of glass came up to Hi'iaka's shoulders. "When the full moon rises, its light will shine through the glass. Kanaloa's magic will magnify and intensify the glow, and it *will* throw your shadow, Little Egg. It will stretch long and deep, and I will stand in it, wash myself in it, and in your moon-shadow, I will drink your *mana* like water."

A dread chill tumbled through her veins. She had never heard of such magic…but Kanaloa was a powerful *akua* of sorcery, and if any could infuse the lens with the ability to throw moonglow like sunlight, it was him. "Why would the god of the underworld and magic help you?" she whispered.

The pig-god laughed. "Why would he help me? Why *wouldn't* he help me? The families of Kāne and Pele have kept Kanaloa buried beneath the earth for millennia. While we bask in the sunshine, he grows bitter and cold in the caverns of death. The status quo punishes him cruelly. What would he *not* give to upset it?"

"A change of order is one thing. But you think Kanaloa will let you destroy *nā akua* and take power over the islands? You think he will not see your vileness and cast such magic on you that *you* become the one locked away beneath the ground? You think he would let Hawai'i fall to sadistic ruin because he bears a grudge against Kāne? Kanaloa may be embittered, but he is not stupid."

"Well," the pig-god said, his teeth gleaming dangerously in the dying light, "stupid enough to think I would actually allow him access to the upside."

Hi'iaka laughed once, a hard, cold burst. "You are meddling with such strengths as you cannot possibly hope to defeat."

"*Tsk-tsk-tsk*," Kamapuaʻa said, shaking his head in mock injury. "It is as if you do not listen to a word I say."

"Your plan will not work," Hiʻiaka insisted, but her words trembled with doubt. "No *akua* has ever had her *mana* stolen by shadow magic. You are a fool, and you will fail."

Kamapuaʻa lifted his eyes to the setting sun. "Well," he said, giving a little shrug, "soon enough, we will see."

# Chapter 23

Gray was tired, and hungry, and he couldn't hold out much longer.

He hadn't eaten since the mangos at the fallen tree. His stomach snarled; his blood sugar had hit a new low, and his mental and emotional anguish had frayed his nerves down to sparking wires. His legs were sore from the climb through the impenetrable terrain, and the world was spinning from exhaustion and hunger and confusion, making it impossible to progress beyond a slow crawl. And on top of everything else, the sun was starting to set, which meant two things: One, he'd been on the mountain for almost twelve hours, which was impossible to process; and two, the full moon would be rising soon, and he was running out of time.

He labored up the pig trail, crawling on his hands and knees at places, digging Manaiakalani into the earth and using it like a mountain climbing pick to pull himself up. He took a tumble over the snarling roots of a tree, hitting the ground chin-first, his teeth clacking painfully in his head. He groaned and rolled over onto his side, ready to just lie there until the end. But he turned and saw the grass was dotted with small, greenish fruit from the tree. He didn't recognize it, but his stomach grumbled, and he thought, *Well... death by poison can't be worse than death by half-pig demigod.*

He picked one up and took a bite. It was sour, and sharp, and the flavor of it rang through his mouth in an uncomfortable sort of way. But it also quenched his thirst, and when he swallowed it, his stomach greedily demanded more. He pulled himself to his knees and gathered up as many of the fruits as he could. He pulled them all back and leaned up against the trunk of the tree, shoving the fruit into a pile between his legs. He held one green ball in each hand and bit into them, gorging himself, stuffing his mouth so full he couldn't breathe. He choked down his sour saviors and picked up two more fruit, tearing into them just as hungrily.

When it was all said and done, he'd eaten nine of the apple-sized fruits, and his stomach felt like it might burst.

"Thank you, tree," he whispered, closing his eyes and resting his head against the bark. "The rain brings trees, and the trees bring food." It wasn't exactly Polunu's Hawai'ian saying, but it was tribute enough, and true.

Gray pushed himself back up to his feet. The light was dying; he needed to hurry. The fruit had re-energized him; the horizon was no longer spinning, and the ground seemed firmer and his feet less cumbersome beneath him. He tightened his grip on Maui's hook and hurried up the hill, plowing through the growth and moving as fast as his legs would allow.

And then, within seconds, he heard the unmistakable chorus of snorting pigs and spied the light of a bonfire through the bushes.

He had come to the trail's end.

He crept up behind a dark green bush with wide leaves and peered around the edge, holding Manaiakalani at the ready. The bonfire threw the long shadows of pigs into the forest. They seemed to be dancing wild circles around a man wearing only a piece of animal hide around his waist and what looked like an elaborate head-dress over his entire head. But as the man jerked closer to the fire, Gray saw with growing dread and terror that it wasn't a headdress at all. It was his actual *head*…the head of a giant boar.

It was Kamapua'a, the half-pig god.

"He's not so big," Gray whispered aloud. But there was no point trying to trick his brain; the demigod was built like a professional athlete, with the added bonus of sporting three-inch tusks out of each side of his mouth. He was at least a full head taller than Gray, probably more, and the pig-god outweighed the mainlander by at least a good 50 pounds of muscle and sweat. "What am I doing here, what am I doing here, what am I doing here?" Gray hissed in a panic. Manaiakalani suddenly felt like it weighed a ton.

But then he looked beyond the pig-god, and there, in the center of the clearing, stood Hi'iaka. The wind whipped through her dark, shining hair, winding it around her shoulders. She wore a blue silk dress, and even though it was torn at the hem and splattered with mud, and even though she looked tired and raw, and even though her back was bowed with defeat and her lips pursed in despair, she was radiant. The setting sun framed her shoulders, and the tips of her hair were alight with the fire of the sky. Her honey brown skin shone with a rosy glow in the crackling firelight, and her eyes held such a fierceness and depth that he lost his heart all over again.

He smelled it, then, the coconut-vanilla scent of her. It carried across the clearing on the breeze and filled his lungs. His heart began to race, his mind was cleared of its clouds, and he felt strength surge through his veins.

And with that strength came hope.

"Hi'iaka," he whispered, breathing her name across the leaves.

She looked up. She squinted into the dying light. She locked eyes with him and gasped. Tears sprang into her eyes, and she gave her head a little shake, wiping the tears away with the tips of her fingers. And then she lowered her head, dropping her chin to her chest, and she smiled.

Something in that smile set off a charge.

"*AAAHHHHH!!!*" Gray exploded through the bush and screamed a warrior's cry as he sprinted at the pig-god, Manaiaka-lani held high.

Then he tripped on a half-buried stone, lost his footing, and went sprawling face-first into the squealing herd of pigs.

The boars screamed with anger and excitement. As Gray plunged into their circle, they attacked, stamping his fingers beneath their hooves and thrusting their tusks against his skin. Gray cried out in agony until the rumble of a deep, rich laughter reached a crescendo over the din of the pigs, and the crushing and stabbing subsided. The boars retreated and drew themselves into a tight circle around the rumpled, injured human lying in the mud and whimpering against his wounds.

The laugher rang through the mountain. Kamapua'a stepped through the ring of hogs, his ribs shaking with the force of his delight. He approached Gray and crouched down to one knee. He grabbed the human's chin with one hand and pinched, hard. Gray squeaked in pain, and Kamapua'a lowered his terrible boar's head so that Gray could see the wet blackness in his wild eyes and smell the rotten meat on his breath. "So here is Pele's army," the pig-god snarled, turning Gray's head from side to side and inspecting it carefully. "You are more pathetic than I could have possibly imagined." He released his grip on Gray's jaw, and Gray sank down to the ground.

"And she armed you with this!" Kamapua'a continued gleefully, reaching down and plucking Manaiakalani from the earth. He held it up to the last rays of the sun; even after all the distress, and despite the barnacles that still clung to its surface, the bone gleamed in the light like a polished gem. "Manaiakalani. Old Maui's crutch." He laughed heartily and flung the hook down in the mud beside Gray. It stuck straight up in the earth and quivered with power. "Didn't the queen of volcanoes tell you? I am no parcel of land to be dredged up by hooks." He turned toward Hi'iaka and gestured down at the fallen mortal with both hands. "You see what your sister sends? Is it folly, do you think? Or does she truly not care to see you live? Her failure to send real help seems almost intentional."

Gray pushed himself up to his hands and knees. His hands were bruised and bleeding, and his left thumb was either jammed, or broken. He had shallow tusk wounds on both legs, and at least one below his sore ribs. It was a struggle to breathe. Everything hurt; everything bled. The pigs leered at him, hungry for more destruction. They were ravenous, and even if he could best them, their demigod was no trifle. If Gray had come into the clearing with any hope of escaping alive, it had just evaporated like water on a desert rock.

But if he was going out, he was going out hard.

He lunged forward and threw his shoulder into Kamapua'a's shins. The pig-god's legs buckled, and the two men went tumbling to the ground. Kamapua'a laughed, and the ringing, squealing sound of it dug into Gray's skin like tiny shards of glass. He swung his fist up and slammed it into the pig-god's chin. Kamapua'a snorted in surprise, and his teeth snapped together with a loud *crack*, but Gray took the brunt of the pain; the demigod had bones as hard as iron, and Gray's hand popped sickeningly as it crunched into the unyielding skull.

"*Ow!*" he cried, rolling onto his back and shaking the pain from his fist. "What are you *made* of?!"

The pig-god pulled himself up to his feet and sneered down at the mortal. "The brutality of nature, meat-thing. Immortality and the raw strength of the earth."

Gray squeezed his eyes shut tight and flexed his fingers. "Did you just call me 'meat-thing'?" he asked.

"Gray!" The voice this time was Hi'iaka's, sharp as cracking crystal. "Look out!"

Gray opened his eyes just in time to see Kamapua'a's bare foot rushing down at his neck from above. He cried out and spun to his side as the demigod's heel stomped down into the earth, leaving a shallow crater that had almost been Gray's flattened trachea. Gray reached out and grabbed Maui's hook. He tried to roll away, but the circle of snarling pigs shouldered him back into the ring. He clamored to his feet and danced away from their gleaming tusks. "Hi'iaka!" Gray shouted desperately to his left, not taking his eyes from the advancing Kamapua'a. "Any chance of a little help?"

Hi'iaka placed a palm against her forehead and closed her eyes as tears spilled down her cheeks. "I can't," she said quietly, and Gray felt his heart break inside of her words.

"Well, that really sucks," he mumbled.

The demigod stalked closer, grinning beneath his snout, drooling down his own belly. He circled around the mainlander, giving him a wide berth, enjoying the moment. "You are playing an important role in history, mainlander. I wonder if you appreciate that. Once the moon rises and captures the Little Egg in its light, the very essence of this world will shift." The sun had sunk completely behind the horizon now, and the sky was slowly plunging into its velvet-blue darkness. The first stars had already twinkled to life high above the mountain, and the moon wouldn't be far behind. "Soon," the pig-god grinned. "With the *mana* of Hi'iaka, I will extinguish Pele. I will bind Nāmaka with ropes of barbed wire. I will lock Kāne in a box and drown him in the ocean. I will tear down the thrones of Wakea and Papa and chain them to the spirits of the underworld. I will slit Maui's throat with the bones of a fish. I will rip each *akua* from his place beneath the sun and drown him beneath the waters of my whim. And when I alone remain, I will demand great sacrifice from the people of Hawai'i. They will laud me with beasts and bloodthirsty games. And when they disappoint me, I will pluck their limbs from their trunks and sprinkle the valleys with their blood. I am Kamapua'a, and my power will be absolute."

"Yeah, I got it—you're gonna destroy the world," Gray said through gritted teeth. "Can we just get it over with?"

"I do not think we are done," Kamapua'a sneered.

But Gray was. He lunged at the demigod. He swung Manaiaka-lani, hard. It sang like steel as it sliced through the air. Gray brought it down hard against Kamapua'a's neck...but the demigod tilted his head at just the last moment, and the point of the hook collided with his tusk. The bones rang out like two boulders being smashed together, and the shock from the force of it dislocated Gray's shoulder. He screamed in pain and dropped the great Hook of Maui. He fell back to his knees and clutched at his shoulder, whimpering and cursing. He looked up and locked eyes with Hi'iaka, who had gone ghostly pale. She buried her mouth against her hands and shook her head in helpless disbelief.

Gray struggled to keep his voice even as he said, "I'm sorry. I tried."

Hi'iaka lowered her trembling hands and placed them over her heart. "No," she whispered. "*I* am sorry. I am so sorry, Grayson Park."

"You are both sorry," the pig-god sneered. "But see how impatiently the moon rises." He gestured up into the sky with his snout, and indeed, the moon had already begun its ascension into the sky. "*Now*, mainlander, I think we are done."

The lens atop the pole caught the moon's light, and Hi'iaka was horrified to see the glow intensify and focus into a soft, luminescent beam that struck the dirt at her feet. She backed up to the far edge of her circle, as far as she could go, but as the moon rose, the light crept closer. In just a few minutes, it would cast her shadow, and Kamapua'a would step into it, draining her of her strength and doubling his own. There was no doubt now that it would happen as he predicted; the glowing beam of moonlight on the dirt thrummed with the unmistakable power of Kanaloa's magic.

The *akua* of the underworld had bargained with the pig-lord and doomed them all.

"So we have run out of time." Kamapua'a hooked his foot beneath Manaiakalani and kicked it back, flinging it away and far out of reach.

Gray clutched his right arm as he struggled painfully to his feet. If he was going to get eaten by a half-pig demigod, he was going to do it with some dignity. "You won't get away with this," he said, though he was pretty sure it wasn't true. It just seemed like the right sort of thing to say.

Kamapua'a placed his hands on Gray's shoulders. Gray cringed and tried not to shrink away, but the demigod was terrible to behold, and he smelled even worse. He pulled his head away, but Kamapua'a nuzzled forward and brushed his tusks along Gray's cheek. "It has been many ages since a human has made a sacrifice of himself to me. I have missed the flavor of submission." He licked at his hog lips, and Gray squirmed as a stream of festering saliva splattered against his temple. "Before you die, it is important that you know that you have been absolutely insignificant. Your life has meant little, even now at the end. And your death...it means nothing at all."

Then he lunged forward, and Gray fell beneath his teeth; the fleshy, sunken sound of bone plunging into skin filled his ears as the world went dark.

Even the pigs fell silent as their demigod feasted.

That darkness and that silence lasted for several very long seconds before Grayson realized he didn't feel any pain.

*This is what it's like to be dead,* he thought.

Then he opened his eyes.

Kamapua'a still stood before him, his swinish chin hairs bristling against Gray's skin. But his eyes were wide and bulging, and the spittle that dripped from his tusks was now frothy and tinged with pink.

Gray looked down.

The tip of Maui's hook jutted out from Kamapua'a's stomach, dripping scarlet beads of blood.

Gray stared at the demigod's wound, stunned. Kamapua'a coughed and sputtered. A thick, azure liquid spilled out from the hole in his abdomen, mixing with the blood and spreading into a purple between his feet.

Gray leaned to the side and looked around at Kamapua'a's back. Hi'iaka stood behind him, fierce in the flickering light of the fire, the handle of Manaiakalani clutched tightly in her hands. She stepped up closer to the half-pig demigod and bared her teeth. "The games of *nā akua* are not yours to play, half-god." Then she twisted the hook, pulled hard, and ripped it back out of his body. The life and divinity flowed out of him like water.

The boars began to back away. They shook their heads and twitched their ears, pawed at their snouts with their great, dirty hooves, and backed into the forest. They turned and disappeared into the brush, squealing and snorting and leaving their god to bleed.

Kamapua'a's head began to sag. His cheeks drooped, and his snout began to melt down over his tusks. The hairs fell out of his chin, and his ears withered down and shriveled up against the sides of his skull. The splotchy black pigment faded into nutshell brown, and his skin melted and warped until it had reformed itself into his human face.

He staggered around to face Hi'iaka. His eyes were round with shock, and the blood that dripped from his lips was frothing with anger. "Little Egg..." he hissed.

She stepped up close, the fire of her eyes boring into his. "I told you I would break you like a shell," she said through clenched teeth. "You should have taken better care with your words. And your deeds." She lifted her hands into the air, still grasping the red and dripping Manaiakalani. She moved her lips, chanting a silent song, and clouds gathered in the night sky. They grew black and ominous, and within seconds, lightning crackled to life above the storm, flashing through the clouds and spreading to all horizons. A bolt shot down and cracked against the pane of magic glass, shattering it into molten drops of sand. The sound was deafening, and Gray clapped his hands to his ears and prayed—*prayed*—that he wasn't wetting himself again. Two more bolts crackled down and struck on either side of Kamapua'a, scorching the earth at his feet and bubbling the pools of blood and divinity that were spreading through the grass. "Go, Kamapua'a. Go, Lord of No Pigs. Crawl into the woods like an animal and die quietly beneath the frail leaves of your kukui trees. There is no more place for you on Maui; you do not deserve, nor will you receive, the mercy of Hawai'i."

The electric storm raged overhead, and fear filled Kamapua'a's eyes. He clutched his stomach and stumbled back, falling speechlessly into the upcountry wild. He tried to drag himself back up to his feet, to summon his strength, to stem the loss of his own *mana*, but his body failed him, slowly draining itself of its immortality, and his legs gave out beneath him. He crawled away on his elbows and knees, whimpering with the incredulity of pain, and he pulled himself up to the river's edge. He reached up, as if grasping for some hidden rope to pull him over the water.

Then he toppled headfirst into the raging waters and was washed away into the crushing falls below.

# Chapter 24

"What…just happened?"

Gray swooned, as much from exhaustion and shock as from overall blood loss, and Hi'iaka caught him, wrapping an arm around his waist and helping him stand tall. "You saved me, Grayson Park," she said, her eyes shining and a smile spreading across her lips. Her wind chime voice had returned, and the very sound of it soothed his breath.

He shook his head, trying to clear some sense into his brain. "I don't…no, *you* saved *me*."

Hi'iaka nodded with a smile. "We seem to have saved each other."

Gray leaned on her support, and the scent of her overpowered his senses. He filled himself with it until he was coursing with coconut and vanilla from the tips of his toes to the ends of his hair. It gave him strength, and he stood straighter, though he didn't lift his arm from around her shoulders. "But you said…you said you couldn't help. And it was *real*, you were…I mean, you *couldn't*." He remembered the crack that splintered his heart when she'd said the words.

"I couldn't. I was contained. I was trapped in the pig-god's circle. But you brought Manaiakalani. You brought a tool of the gods, imbued with such power...didn't you see?" Hi'iaka laughed. It was the sound of birds chirping amid the rumble of a summer storm.

Gray shook his head. "See what?" he asked.

"When you dropped Manaiakalani on the ground...the pig-god kicked it aside. Didn't you see?"

Gray closed his eyes and furrowed his brow. He was trying desperately to follow along. "No. I mean, I saw him kick it, yes, but...?"

"He kicked it into my circle. Manaiakalani hit the ground and slid through the dirt, wiping a blank space through the line, breaking my prison. You brought the key to my cell, Grayson," she said, taking his face in her hands. "And Kamapua'a himself turned it in the lock."

"Oh." Gray blinked. Then he blinked again. He felt a smile curl up at the corners of his lips as he melted into her touch. "Well...I mean...it was Pele's idea to get the hook," he said, shrugging modestly.

"My sister has great love for me," Hi'iaka nodded, brushing the tips of her fingers along Gray's cheek. "I have never doubted that, not truly. But she has her responsibilities, and you...you were the one to see it through." Her cheeks burned crimson, then, and she glanced away as she added, "Just like I had hoped you would be."

Gray smiled...but as the scent of her became a thing less potent, the reality of the last few days rushed back to him. "I..." he began. But a lump rose up in his throat, blocking the words. Tears welled up in his eyes, and he pressed his forehead into Hi'iaka's hair. "I...I lost a...a friend." The word was so completely inadequate that his neck burned with the shame of it. "Not a friend. Not even family. Something...different. Something bigger. I don't know the word for it." The tears spilled over, and a shaking sob wracked his chest. "I lost a Polunu," he wept quietly. "I lost my Polunu."

Hi'iaka burrowed her face into his chest. "I know," she whispered. "I know. I am so sorry, Grayson." She dabbed her own tears on the collar of his shirt. "I am sorry for being the cause of—"

"No," he said curtly, cutting her off. "It wasn't you. Coming here was what he wanted. He believed all along. He knew, and he believed, and he wouldn't stop until it was made right. And because of him, we *did* make it right." He lifted his head and snuffled as he wiped his nose on his sleeve. "It's just—he was—he—"

Hi'iaka placed a palm on Gray's chest. "He was your 'ohana, Grayson."

Gray laughed, a short, sad burst, his eyes working to blink back his tears and proving themselves unequal to the task. "It's stupid, I literally did not know him at all. I don't—"

"He was your 'ohana," she said again, more firmly. "And we will not forget him."

Something inside of Gray broke, something tucked deep inside his heart, and he began to sob. "No," he said, wiping his face with his hands and trying to control his breath, "we will not."

They stood there together like that until the moon was high in the nighttime sky, clinging to each other, wiping their tears and sharing their smiles and not really knowing how to feel, but feeling it all the same.

# Chapter 25

Kamapua'a heaved himself out of the water, his fingers digging into the mud and pulling his trailing body up the shore.

His body had been slammed through three separate falls, churned against the river's floor, and battered against its boulders. But he was a demigod, and broken bones were for mortals.

Still…as he lay there wheezing against the silt, he felt a splinter in his side, and blood now trickled from his head and his elbow in addition to the wound in his belly, which still leaked a strange and unfamiliar mixture of scarlet red and azure blue. His skin had never before suffered a puncture wound, and he was somewhat surprised to see his own blood, but immensely intrigued at the sight of the blue fluid. He had never seen any being, mortal or immortal, weep bright blue blood from a wound, and it mesmerized him. *This blue is a thing of power*, he reasoned. *It belongs to Kamapua'a alone, and it flows from me now as a sign that I shall rise again and take vengeance on my enemies.* And the number of his enemies was growing by the day.

Still, he felt dizzy…weak. Those were things he had never felt before.

And he could not transform into his true face.

That was concerning, too.

He crawled up the shore, pulling himself from the water by the roots of the *pili* grass that grew along the bank. Safe from the current's pull, he rolled over onto his back and pressed his hand once more to the wound on his belly, urging the blood to stop flowing.

*Maui kept his hook sharper than I gave him credit for,* he thought, pressing into the gash. The old man was earning a higher rank on Kamapua'a's list.

He lay there on the bank for many minutes, collecting his strength and willing the bloods, both red and blue, to stop flowing. And finally, the azure fluid did stop. It dripped its final drops onto the grass, and Kamapua'a felt himself emptied of the substance, and he decided to count himself lucky. Sign of power or not, a foreign body in the bloodstream can only prove bothersome, he concluded, and he was well rid of the strangely-colored stuff.

And yet...he felt so strange, so weary, so bone-tired now, the way he had always imagined a mortal must feel, locked within a chamber of withering skin and moldering bone, and Kamapua'a wondered if the azure blood had anything to do with that.

He had only just pulled himself to his knees when he heard the beat of a distant drum.

He cocked his head and listened intently. The sound was unmistakable; it was being played in the style of the ancients, the slow, methodical way the warriors would beat a tattoo while they marched between their battles for the islands. The sound of the drum grew louder, drew nearer, until it was just beyond the trees and still moving his way.

A shimmering blue light began to glow beyond the woods. The Lord of Pigs squinted his eyes to see better in the darkness, something he had never needed to do before. And in the gloaming, he saw the withering shapes of ghostly blue warriors marching slowly between the trees, their faces drawn in mournful remembrance, their steps heavy and plodding, weary and spent.

It was the Night Marchers, tangled in their eternal search for the gateway to the life beyond.

Kamapua'a sneered as he dragged himself to his feet. As a demigod, he was immune to their curse, and he felt somehow scorned by their appearance on this shore, on this mountain, on this island, as if this place were for the pig-god alone, and the other demons and ghosts of Hawai'i should know to pay homage to his solitude.

He drew himself up to his full height as they marched nearer, though it caused him a slicing pain in his belly that he had never thought possible. The Night Marchers came on, beating the drum and stepping in time, and he stared them down, knowing that after all he'd been through, after the inexplicable blow dealt by the Little Egg and her mainlander whelp, and after his temporarily-failed attempt to double his strength and establish dominance over the gods, he could still wield power over at least some of the other-worldly forces that haunted the islands. And so he stood, tall and proud, and he looked the ghostly soldiers in the eye and snidely ushered them past.

But three of the soldiers broke rank when they approached his place on the shore. They floated toward him, their eyes sunken to black holes, their mouths gaping and slack. They dared approach Kamapua'a, the greatest demigod of the Polynesian realm, and they reached out for him with their ghastly, ghostly fingers. He withdrew in repulsion, and commanded them, "Back to your rank-and-file, cretins." But still they reached, and their hollow fingers seized upon his wrists, and he gasped and tried to pull away, but they held him tight. "Release me!" he screamed, but the ghosts would not relent. They began to retreat, and they dragged him from the grass at the edge of the river, pulling him down into the host of ghouls. "Unhand me!" Kamapua'a screeched, struggling against their grip. "I am *akua*! I am your god! Release me, or you will pay the price!"

But the Night Marchers felt for his immortality and found it drained away. Kamapua'a was no longer the half-man, half-pig demigod of Hawai'i. He was a mortal man, wounded and sick, half-drowned and half-dead, and he had dared to lock eyes with the soldiers of death's army.

The truth dawned upon Kamapua'a too late. He screamed as the ghosts dragged him into their line, and then he was swallowed up by the dead, lost forever, another slack-mouthed ghost with hollowed eyes, one of so many Night Marchers, endlessly wandering for the rest of all eternity.

# Chapter 26

Hi'iaka melted into her sister's embrace. She glowed red with the heat of Pele's fire, then she became soft and rendered down into lava. The two sisters became one swirling column of burning magma, little jets of fire bursting from all sides. Then they pulled away and reformed into themselves, solid and whole and beaming and radiant.

Gray found he needed to sit down.

"You are safe, Little Egg," Pele said, caressing her sister's cheek tenderly. The lava surrounding them surged triumphantly into the air. Gray pulled his feet back from the edge and tried not to get splashed.

"Thanks to you, sister," Hi'iaka replied, clasping Pele's hands in her own. "And thanks to Grayson."

Pele turned toward the human in surprise, as if she had just now realized that he was there. "Yes, mainlander. You succeeded admirably. My sister chose you well."

"And you still burned me," he said, working his injured shoulder.

Pele smirked. "You lacked motivation and required encouragement. But in the end, you did very well."

"I...I didn't do it alone." Gray's hands trembled, and he fussed at the hem of his shirt to keep them busy. "Polunu...he was..." He cleared his throat, blinked back his tears, and began again. "Pol-unu…helped. But he…he fell."

Pele lowered her eyes and nodded. "Yes. I know. Your friend was a brave soul. He had a good heart, and a fierce love of Hawai'i. We will honor him."

"We will," Hi'iaka confirmed, patting Gray's hand.

"I know," he said, giving up a weak smile. "We will." He sniffled and wiped his nose on his sleeve. "I need to…find his family, or something. Tell them what happened."

"I will handle that task," Pele said. "I set him on the journey; the responsibility is mine."

"Oh. Okay. That's great." He nodded awkwardly. "Thank you."

"I will send my *mo'o* to seek out his 'ohana."

Gray leapt to his feet. "What?!"

But Hi'iaka squeezed his hand reassuringly. "Not all *mo'o* are evil, Grayson. Many are good spirits, and kind. They will be apt for the task."

Gray shook his head. "I just do not understand Hawai'ian my-thology," he mumbled.

"There is plenty of time to learn." A smile played on Hi'iaka's lips, and her eyes danced in the light of the swirling lava.

"You returned Manaiakalani to Maui?" Pele asked, cutting them short.

"Yes," Gray nodded. "We did."

"And he was grateful?"

Gray frowned. "He said we should have thrown it into the river with Kamapua'a and let it be washed out to the center of the ocean."

"But his little sea monsters were happy to have a purpose again," Hi'iaka added cheerfully.

"All is well, then. Mainlander, it is nearly sunrise, and you must be exhausted, being mortal and weak of flesh."

Gray frowned. "Umm…well…I *am* tired. I'm not…I mean, I wouldn't say I'm *weak* of flesh…" He instinctively rubbed his shoulder, which still hurt, even though Hi'iaka had reset it. He hoped she wouldn't bring it up.

"You must go now, and rest. Restore your energy, and be satisfied in the feat you have accomplished. It is no small thing to face a demigod; you have aided greatly in the salvation of Hawai'i, and you will forever be counted as a friend of the islands."

"Thank you." Then Grayson bowed, because he felt like he should do *something*, but maybe a bow wasn't it, because it was a stiff bow, and awkward, and he wished he hadn't tried it at all.

Pele turned to Hi'iaka. "Sister…would that I could have raged against Kamapua'a myself. But my responsibilities here…" She let her words drift, and a current of regret ran beneath them.

But Hi'iaka held up her hand. "I know that what you do here is a great sacrifice, and a greater burden. I did not wish to distract you from it, sister. I know full well what Nāmaka would do if you left your cauldron for even a moment. All I needed was for you to set the humans on their course, and you did. You are ever my loving sister." She kissed Pele's cheek, and Pele returned the embrace.

"And you, my Little Egg," the volcano goddess whispered.

Hi'iaka smiled. "Be well, Pele-honua-mea. I will see you soon."

Then she stepped out of the lava pool and disappeared through the doorway, beckoning with a nod for Grayson to follow.

"Mainlander," Pele said, stopping Gray short before he could take a step.

"Yeah?" He coughed and cleared his throat. "Erm. Yes? Ma'am?"

Pele raised an eyebrow in his direction. "Be gentle with your attachment to my sister. Remember that you are mortal; you will grow old, become crippled, wither, die, and blow away to dust while my sister but blinks her eye."

Gray swallowed. "Well. That's…a nice image."

"I have said all I need to say. Thank you for your courage and your assistance, Grayson Park. May you forever be well." And the volcano goddess melted into her lava pit, disappearing once more between the burning, roiling fire.

҆

"Your sister's pretty intense," Gray said.

They stood on the deck outside of the resort, watching the moon fade in the early morning sky.

Hi'iaka grinned. "She is…rigid," the goddess assented. "But surely not so terrifying as all that."

"She *literally* made me wet myself." Hi'iaka laughed her wind chime laugh, and it rang through the air and the salty ocean breeze. Gray grinned and shook his head. "I definitely should *not* have just told you that," he decided.

"You would keep a secret from me, Grayson Park of Missouri?" she said, feigning astonishment. She leaned back with her elbows on the railing. They were both dirty, disheveled, covered in mud and blood and crusted blue stains of divinity, but no woman in history had ever looked as majestic as Hi'iaka looked to Gray in that moment.

"*That* kind of secret? I should probably start," he said with a smile. "And that's who I am, now? Grayson Park of Missouri? After all this, *that's* my official title?"

"You don't like it?" she grinned.

"It's not my favorite."

"*Tsk-tsk-tsk*," Hi'iaka clucked. "I should have fled to Moloka'i after all."

"Maybe," Grayson agreed. "But then you'd still be having nightmares. And Kampua'a would still be a problem."

"Mm. That is true." Hi'iaka took his hand and rubbed at a smear of dried blood with her thumb. "I wonder what I will dream of tonight," she said.

Gray laughed, a nervous little explosion that made Hi'iaka giggle. "Listen, is this...are we—? I mean, I know this is stupid, because I'm just a person, and you're immortal, and Pele was like, 'Hey, hands off,' and I am *definitely* on the rebound, and that's never a good time for this sort of thing, but...I mean, there *is* something here...right?"

Hi'iaka shifted closer so that their elbows touched, and once again, Grayson felt that surging warmth spread through his arm. "Time and the wind connect all manner of things, mortal and immortal alike," she said gently, brushing her fingertips along the back of his hand. "Fire and water are unlikely companions, yet when they meet, islands are born." She lifted her eyes, boring them into Grayson's. "We have a connection. I do not know yet the width or breadth of it...but I would choose to find out."

Gray smiled, and his shoulders melted into butter. He bumped his forehead gently against hers. "I leave Maui in four days," he whispered.

Hi'iaka smiled. "Time and space are simply foes to be conquered," she said. "It is not so hard to do. Not if you know how. And I will tell you the secret." She brought her lips to his ears and whispered, "*Kö aloha lä 'ea, kö aloha lä 'ea.*"

Grayson smiled. "You know, I've heard that before," he said, brushing her cheek with his lips. "I think it sounds like pretty good advice."

The moon faded in the light of the rising sun as he kissed her, and in a warm Hawai'ian wind of pineapple, vanilla, coconut, and salt, they began their fight against space and time.

# Epilogue

The goddess sat on her sea-glass throne, and the ocean broke across her feet. "How did the pig-lord's trick play out, Ka-moho-ali'i?" she asked, her voice crashing like the waves.

The shark god lifted himself from the water and stood fiercely atop the roiling sea. "As you said it would, Nāmaka." Then he added, "More or less."

Nāmaka nodded slowly, letting her thoughts tumble freely as she skimmed a hand across the surface of the ocean. "Kamapua'a has ever been a fool," she declared.

"Now he is a ghostly fool," Ka-moho-ali'i said, showing his sharp, triangular teeth with a wide shark's grin. "Your sister drained him of his divinity, and he was taken by the Night Marchers."

Nāmaka raised an eyebrow at that. "Truly?" she asked. The shark god nodded. "How unexpected," she mused. "How wonderfully fascinating."

"It was Maui's hook that did the draining."

Nāmaka's brow darkened. "Maui. The great trickster, gone long into hiding, has finally chosen a side, has he?" She gritted her teeth. "He has chosen poorly."

Ka-moho-ali'i remained silent, but mischief gleamed in his eyes.

"Kamapua'a's failure is disappointing, but not surprising," Nā-maka continued. "If his little game had lured Pele away from her chamber, he would have saved me much effort. But then, the effort is the fun of it all, don't you think?"

Ka-moho-ali'i nodded. "Yes, sister. I do."

She lifted a stone jug from the base of her throne and held it lightly between her hands. The shark god stiffened, and his breathing became labored.

"What of the mortal?" she asked, running her finger along the lip of the jar.

"The mainlander?" the shark god asked, his focus waning.

"No. The other one. The fat one."

"Polunu."

"Yes, this Polunu. Did you find him?"

"I did," Ka-moho-ali'i nodded.

"Is he dead?"

"Completely."

"Was he taken to the underworld?"

"No," the shark god said proudly, thumping a fin against his chest. "I found him in time."

"Good." Nāmaka brought forth a corral cup from the water and poured a measure of 'awa from the jug. She handed it to the shark god, who snatched it greedily and drank it down in one swallow. He instantly relaxed, and his eyes rolled back a bit, and an uneven smile crept across his face. Nāmaka retrieved the cup and set it and the jar back into the sea. "Go down below the world and speak with Kanaloa. Bargain to keep the fat one's body, and for whatever sorcery Kanaloa must use should I wish to bring him back. This human may yet have a role to play."

The shark god snorted. "The role of mortals is to serve as food," he said, his voice fluid and soft.

"Generally, I agree with you," Nāmaka said. "But Hiʻiaka is Pele's weakness, and the mainlander may be Hiʻiaka's. *Nā akua* may not be easy to topple, but this mortal, Grayson Park…though he has proven himself surprisingly resourceful, I think he will be the key to bringing down my sister. Crush that stone, and the whole tower will fall. The fat one—this Polunu—will be the chisel." She tented her fingers over her chest and smiled a wicked grin. "And I will be the hammer."

Ka-moho-aliʻi bowed low, scraping his belly against the reef.

"Go now to Kanaloa. Secure his commitment and allegiance. Tell him to wait for my call, for we will bide our time until opportunity is ripe. And that," the goddess hissed, gripping the arms of her throne and baring her teeth at her sister's volcano, looming in the distance, "is when Nāmaka will have her revenge."

# Acknowledgements

Thank you to my wife, Paula, for not only being a daily inspiration to me in every single thing she does, but also for inspiring this book and the magic that lives inside it. I don't know anyone who works as hard or lives so fiercely, and I hope this book captures even a fraction of her spirit. *Aloha nui loa*, Paula.

Thanks also to the incomparable Steven Luna, who kept Gray and Polunu on track when they tried to veer off to nonsensical parts unknown. Steven's love for and dedication to this book might even rival my own, and I can't thank him enough for that. Here's to a whole series of adventures with *nā akua, hoa pili*.

I tried to keep the magic and adventure in this story as close to true Hawaiian mythology as I could. For that, I turned to a lot of questionable online sources, and a few much more solid, wonderful books, including *Hawaiian Mythology* by Martha Beckwith and *The Water of Kāne* by Mary Kawena Pūku'i and Caroline Curtis. I wish they were all still around for me to send my sincerest thanks; their books helped me immensely, and I believe they will continue to be a great resource to me as I continue with the Nā Akua series. I am grateful to all of them for their invaluable guidance.

Finally, thank you to the people of Hawai'i for always being so kind and welcoming when we visit. This book is as much for the Hawai'ian people as it is for anyone else, and I hope I've done their home and their culture justice. I owe much to Hawai'i. *Mahalo nui loa.*

# Author's Note

**IF YOU ENJOYED THIS BOOK,** please take a moment to leave a review on Amazon. Reviews really do make or break the success of a book for independent authors, and your support would be truly and greatly appreciated.

For more information on the specific ways Amazon reviews help make books more successful, visit:

**WWW.STATEOFCLAYTON.COM/WHY-REVIEW**

# About the Author

Photo by Emily Rose Studios

**CLAYTON SMITH** is a writer of speculative fiction who would very much like to move to Hawaii. For now, he lives in Chicago, and that's a nice place, too.

He would love to hear from you! You can visit him online at StateOfClayton.com, or you can find him on Facebook, Twitter, and Instagram as @claytonsaurus.

# Also by Clayton Smith

## APOCALYPTICON

Three years have passed since the Jamaicans caused the apocalypse, and things in post-Armageddon Chicago have settled into a new kind of normal. Unfortunately, that "normal" includes collapsing skyscrapers, bands of bloodthirsty maniacs, and a dwindling cache of survival supplies. After watching his family, friends, and most of the non-sadistic elements of society crumble around him, Patrick decides it's time to cross one last item off his bucket list.

He's going to Disney World.

This hilarious, heartfelt, gut-wrenching odyssey through post-apocalyptic America is a pilgrimage peppered with peril, as fellow survivors Patrick and Ben encounter a slew of odd characters, from zombie politicians and deranged survivalists to a milky-eyed oracle who doesn't have a lot of good news. Plus, it looks like Patrick may be hiding the real reason for their mission to the Magic Kingdom...

## ANOMALY FLATS

Somewhere just off the interstate, in the heart of the American Midwest, there's a quaint, quirky town where the stars in the sky circle a hypnotic void....where magnetic fields play havoc with time and perception...where metallic rain and plasma rivers and tentacles in the plumbing are simply part of the unsettling charm.

Mallory Jenkins is about to experience the unique properties of this place for herself when she accidentally sets off a series of events that could unleash the ultimate evil upon the town and wreak havoc on the world at large.

Life in a small town is like that sometimes.

Welcome to Anomaly Flats. Have some waffles, meet the folks, and enjoy the scenery…and if you happen to be in Walmart, whatever you do, don't go down aisle 8.

Don't EVER go down aisle 8.


## IT CAME FROM ANOMALY FLATS

The oddest little town in the Midwest has a thousand demented stories to tell…some of them are horrifying enough to send shivers down the strongest of spines. There's the tale of a man whose utter fear of germs sends him plummeting to the depths of depravity, and the victims he takes with him; the story of a couple escaping Missouri to fulfill their California dreams who take an innocent detour and find themselves trapped in the most unexpected of nightmares instead; the legend of a demonic creature who thrives on human flesh, which may be more reality than fiction.

In this first collected volume of chill-inducing stories from everyone's favorite transdimensional town, you'll find reason enough to question your own sanity, even as you try to reassure yourself that things like this only happen in stories.

Don't they?

Welcome back to Anomaly Flats.

How loud can you scream?

## PANTS ON FIRE: A COLLECTION OF LIES

A circus performer leaving behind a trail of ghosts; a castle of bumbling nitwits desperate to prove themselves to King Arthur; a world full of deadly mirrors; a librarian who mistakes Death for a very somber wheat farmer; this pesky little thing called "the Rapture." All these and more pepper the pages of Pants on Fire: A Collection of Lies, a twisted, quirky, macabre world full of hilarious and chilling tales. Equal parts humor and horror, these seventeen surprising stories will leave you thrilled, thrown, and enthralled.

Being lied to has never been so much fun!

## MABEL GRAY AND THE WIZARD
## WHO SWALLOWED THE SUN

*2015 INDIEFAB Book of the Year Award Winner!*

All is not well in Brightsbane, the village of eternal night. An evil wizard—the very wizard who swallowed the sun, in fact—has stolen The Boneyard Compendium, a book of powerful spells that could bring about the destruction of the entire town. When an Elder enlists the orphans of St. Crippleback's Home for Waifs and Strays to help track down the wizard, the ever-intrepid Mabel Gray sets out to find the three keys of bone that unlock the Compendium before the wizard gets his diabolical hands on them.

Armed with only her wit and a frightfully small bit of magic in her pocket, Mabel embarks on an adventure that brings her face-to-face with talking scarecrows, high-ranking monsters, babbling witches, ill-tempered daemons, a riddlesome owl who fancies himself a raven, and more. But the wizard isn't a wizard for nothing, and his evil magic may prove to be more powerful than Mabel ever imagined...